TITLES B⅃

Bonna Mae Chapman

Ages 9-14
Easy read mysteries series

Hanna Rae in

Feel The Fear

Enter The Mask

On the Edge

AN ADULT NOVEL

One Last Chance

Covers on all books are done by
Cody Freeman

IN DANGERS WAY

Bonna Mae Chapman

iUniverse, Inc.
New York   Bloomington

In Dangers Way

The views expressed in this work are solely those of the author and do not necessarily reflect the views of the publisher, and the publisher hereby disclaims any responsibility for them.

iUniverse books may be ordered through booksellers or by contacting:

iUniverse
1663 Liberty Drive
Bloomington, IN 47403
www.iuniverse.com
1-800-Authors (1-800-288-4677)

Because of the dynamic nature of the Internet, any Web addresses or links contained in this book may have changed since publication and may no longer be valid. The views expressed in this work are solely those of the author and do not necessarily reflect the views of the publisher, and the publisher hereby disclaims any responsibility for them.

ISBN: 978-1-4401-2637-6 (pbk)
ISBN: 978-1-4401-2638-3 (ebk)

Printed in the United States of America

iUniverse rev. date: 3/3/2009

ACKNOWLEDGEMENTS

A special thanks to **Cody Freeman** who has listened to many hours of book talk. I want to thank you for your insight into the workings of a good book. You have made such a difference and I really appreciate it. Your talent in doing the book covers makes each book special. Thank you, thank you.

Thank you to my loyal reader **Sheila Rushton**. Your opinion means a great deal to me. I'm so lucky to have your help. Thank you.

Thank you to **Carrie Maclean** for your wisdom in the English language. Your encouraging words keep me going. Thank you.

I would like to thank all the people who read my books and rushed up to me at the mall to tell me how much they loved them. Their feedback was what kept me going.

I would like to thank **Ann MacDougall** for her inspiring phone call after reading my first adult novel. I left the message on my phone for months. Whenever I felt discouraged I would go and listen to her message, her voice and her words. Thank you so much.

Contents

1

MOM'S BABY

"I'M TELLING YOU JEAN, he's going to get hurt again!" My father's deep voice was clearly pressing hard.

I opened my eyes to see a wispy shadow cast over my bedroom walls from the streetlight outside. No longer sound asleep, my nose tickled with the smell of cinnamon toast as the aroma drifted toward my room. The clinking of tea cups in the kitchen was barely noticeable above the muffled sound of mom's voice.

The distant kitchen light creased a line of brightness around the edge of my door. I lay motionless staring at my jeans piled on top of a hump of clothing. My sneakers with the backs flattened had dirt pressed into the groves of the deep treads. The earthy smell of the mud wasn't enough to distract me from listening to the conversation that continued.

Her voice faltered as she attempted to persuade him. "I don't know.... summer camp. Sam's my last one at home. He's my baby."

Mom was trying to reason but losing the battle.

Dad's voice lowered into a soft consoling murmur. "Jean, be reasonable. He's fourteen. Things could have been a lot worse. I'm really afraid that he's going to get hurt again." Pausing as he mellowed his tone, he slurped some tea before his cup clinked into the saucer once more. "I know it will be hard at first but you should be thinking of him."

I wondered, when did love turn to hate. For the most part I didn't mind Dad, but still I had a feeling inside that I was unable to put words to. Was it a noticeable thing or had it always been there between the lines waiting for me to acknowledge the difference.

"That's all I've been thinking about, cause, I'll be lost without him. It's still hard getting used to Hanna Rae being gone." Mom sighed before continuing. "Now with her summer job after college… well; she'll only be home the odd weekend this summer."

I reached up and felt a dry roughness where the gash in my scalp had scabbed over. Course black stitches protruded from the newly growing bristled hair on the side of my head. Lightly running my fingers over them, I counted all fifteen. Gently pushing I could tell the bruised feeling was gone. If it hadn't been for my own stupid mistake last week, solving the case of the missing dogs, I bet nothing would be changing now. I could have slipped anywhere cutting my head. Thing was Mom didn't look at it the same way.

"Jean, for heaven's sake, think of Sam! It would be good for him to have a summer doing fun things, kid things." Dad stood pushing his hands into his pockets jingling his few coins. "I went to summer camp there myself eons ago and loved it. The camp is close to Onslow. It could give him a head start on making some new friends before your move there in late August."

"Ok, I'll speak to him tomorrow." She sighed then blew her nose with a pinched sound. "But you know; I'm still not sure."

Dad hesitated then grunted as he rattled his coins some more. "I know. I don't have any right to say much or change things. You raised him for the first nine years by yourself." Quickly he sped up his speech putting in more of his mellowed compassion. "I've been trying hard to help out, take the strain off you and give you more support with everything."

It was about this time that I noticed my fingernails digging into my palms as I clenched my hands shut. I felt uneasy to think that we would be moving away for good, before September. That was also his idea because his mother's house had been empty for some time just waiting to give us a new start in Onslow. My life, this apartment, everything would only be a memory from then on.

It had been a rough time since early spring with, Connor, my best friend moving away. I didn't understand why so many people had to go west for work. Without Connor everything had changed. My only sister, Hanna Rae, and brother, JC, were off to Dalhousie University. It felt like everyone important to me was leaving. By moments, I was overwhelmed with an empty feeling deep in the pit of my stomach. The move in August made perfect sense to be closer to Hanna Rae and JC. They would be able to take the Acadia bus home more often.

With a thump of the door I knew Dad was gone. Hearing the scuff of Mom's slippers across the floor and the click of the lights meant she was off to bed. The creased line of light around my door was once more replaced with a shadowed feeling from the streetlight as it crept through my thin curtains and over my face.

Rolling over I looked up at the ceiling already feeling disjointed between my past and future. It had been almost five years since my dad's return. I couldn't understand the discomfort I felt around him. Still, I resented that he wanted to send me away. Why did I feel like he should have no rights when it came to me? Gradually I slipped into a restless sleep, tossing and turning the rest of the night.

By morning I was twisted up in my blankets and resembled a tootsie roll. Sitting up I gazed around the small room with the one slanted wall. JC's bed sat across the room neatly made with worn blankets but untouched for weeks now. The shelves that lined the walls had several empty spaces where he cleared away things before going off to university. Everything was the same but different.

I sat on the edge of my bed rethinking the conversation from the night before. Above all odds I hoped that mom would come up with her own reasons to deny dad's idea of sending me to camp.

Reaching over I put my glasses on and pushed my hair down flat. I looked around the room that had been so comforting even since I could remember. Standing up I ran my fingers over the notches on the door frame. The rough gouges showed one side was me and the other was JC. Last March break on my fourteenth birthday we made our usual mark on the door frame. There was only a slight difference between our notches now. Before long even the marks would be only a memory.

The bright sunlight was trying hard to shove its way into my room. I could hear mom's slippers as they scuffed over the floor. Soft music from the radio was mixed with the sound of bacon and eggs splattering spots of grease everywhere. Shaking my head I grabbed my stiff jeans off the pile on the floor. Pushing my feet into the pant-legs I stood up and stretched.

Looking up over the walls and towards my window I realized I had come to grips with moving to Onslow but summer camp, well… I simply wouldn't go. Surely I would be able to convince mom to listen to reason.

"Good morning Mom."

"Good morning Sam. How'd ya sleep?" She grabbed the egg flipper and turned towards the stove.

"Not real good. I heard you and Dad talking last night." My mouth went dry as if stuffed with old socks. I opened the fridge and pulled out a container of orange juice. Holding up the container I asked, "Do you want some too?"

"No thanks, I've got tea." She looked at me with the flipper in her hand dripping grease onto the floor. "I've got to talk to you."

I pointed to the floor, at the growing spot of grease. "No way, to the summer camp idea." I gulped down the orange juice, and then shoved a piece of buttered toast into my mouth.

"Your father is right about going to camp." She bent to wipe the grease up. Tipping her head looking straight into my eyes she stood once more. "It's a great place and it will give you a chance to make some new friends before school starts."

"There's no guarantee that anyone I meet there will be in my school." Stopping in mid thought, my attention was drawn to the deep voice of the radio announcer...

"*News flash….* The police need help identifying an unknown vehicle which was seen in Hopeville last evening. The vehicle is described as being a large army type truck, the back covered with a tarp. One barrel of unknown content fell from the vehicle near Main Street. Anyone with more information concerning this vehicle, please call 555-7829."

Quickly I pulled my red notebook from my pocket and started to scribble down the number. Then I became aware that Mom was now standing over me with her hands on her hips. I looked up into her blue eyes with an explanation. "I needed the number, just in case…I… I notice something."

"Right, right; I've seen that look before." Grabbing the corner of her stained apron she wiped her hands off. She gently took the edge of my chin and tipped it up. Inspecting the stitches on the side of my head changed her lips into a fine hard line. "Nothing you can say will change my mind. Your stitches come out tomorrow and the first of the week, you're going to camp."

I jumped up angry at myself for giving her the determination to pull rank. The chair toppled over as I shoved my plate to one side. "You always take his side. I'm telling you it's not right. He wasn't here for the first nine years. He has no right to tell me what to do?"

"Sam, it's decided, besides he cares about you."

My voice busted out louder even though I tried not to yell. "Yea, where was he all those years. Tell me that Mom. Where was he?"

I stormed towards the door. Ripping my jacket from the hook, I left slamming the door hard behind me.

2

MEMORIES

I TORE AROUND THE corner, sped past the long stretch of blue
and white homes till I reached the school yard. Slowing down
just a bit I noticed five or six little kids at the slides. Suddenly
the feeling of missing this place was very strong. The only place
I had ever called home. I pressed on picking up speed past the
pine trees and swung up the path that led to the subdivisions.
The wind whipped my hair around the edge of my glasses.
Finally I had reached a small familiar pine and maple grove
where Connor and I had spent time through the years.

The sun was peaking through the trees and dappled the
ground with sparkling light. I stopped and looked up to the
top branches of a maple. Grabbing the lower branch I swung
up onto the thick sturdy arms. Reaching up with a familiar
speed, I grabbed the next branch one after the other. Finally
I had no more wind left. The air pumped in and out of my
rib cage creating an overwhelming urge to cry as it pressed
against my temples. Biting my lip I stopped, closed my eyes
and breathed deep.

A light breeze, mingled with the sweet smell of the pines was forcing me to keep my eyes closed. My breathing returned to normal as I looked around and knew within my heart that I was anxious because of the uncertain future that lay ahead. This place was home and would always be special to me.

Thoughts of my Dad crept into my mind. At first I was so pleased to finally have one. Someone to spend time with and do all those father and son things. For the most part none of those things ever showed up. Honestly, he tried but it just didn't cut it with me. I felt like there was a desire to make up for lost time with all the discipline. Living up to what I thought he wanted was almost impossible. Finally, I decided things had been just fine before he entered my life.

I was saddened by the mere thought that perhaps Dad wasn't really needed. All the dreams of the father and son things, faded. Hugging the smooth bark of the maple tree I sat till my mind cleared. I could see the black pavement of the main road, the tops of ordinary homes and in the distance the red mud of the ball field. The feeling of things changing faster than I wanted was crushing.

I listened to the traffic noises in the distance. I never realized I could hear the squeak of the school swings from here. Then looking down I saw two joggers as their sneakers slapped the ground of a well worn path just below my tree. About fifteen feet behind them trotted their loyal dog with his tongue hanging almost to the ground.

Time passed, allowing my anger to ease. I gazed across the way and could see from here the old tree house that Connor and I built. It was in a lower section of maple trees scattered among the pines. The dozen boards were grayed from years of weather. Then my memory slipped back to the time when we ran wild among the trees. I smiled thinking of the grand plans we made there on the few boards we scavenged. It felt like so long ago and even though I spoke to Connor often on MSN, it wasn't the same.

Then as I watched I could see a tuff of hair just above the top board. I dropped to a lower branch until I could clearly see two boys huddled among the boards of my old tree house. It had been many years since Connor and I had moved on to better things. New younger boys had moved into the spot we left. No doubt new adventures and plans were being made.

I watched as my own history played out before my eyes. One of the boys had glasses and black hair and the other like me had a head full of unruly red wire. They talked, with raised voices, about some other kids from school and how they would teach them a lesson. The boy with the red wiry hair had a handful of rocks. Pelting the rocks at some distant target he yelled into the still air. "I'm the king of this castle."

The other boy with the black hair stood still as he watched his buddy vent his anger. "Forget them, they don't matter. I've got something else to do."

He pulled something small from his pocket as he seated himself on the edge of the boards.

"What is it?" The other boy dropped the stones and plunked down beside his friend.

I remembered many days Connor and I tried to solve our problems on the same boards nailed at odd angles to the branches of that maple. Then their voices became very quiet and muffled. I dropped to a lower level in my own tree, till I could see their sneakers dangling down below the boards. Watching closely, I saw smoke puff around the edges of the boards. We had sat in the same spot, history repeating itself.

The memories flooded back to the days that Connor and I had tried smoking. My stomach twisted, I could almost smell the sulfur from the match. Connor snuck a few short pieces of a cigarette from his big brother, John's ashtray. We felt like we were so grown up and wanted a taste of the bigger life. Our curiosity grew until he arrived one day at the tree house with the biggest smile.

"I got us a few wine dipped cigars." He fumbled in his pocket and pulled out two long slender cigars still in the wrapper.

"Oh no, don't you think you'll get caught." I was so foolish to think we could get away with things. Later on we found out John left them for us knowing what would happen. We each sat in the tree house and puffed the whole thing till all that was left was the wine tip.

Connor said, "I wonder if you can get drunk off that thing?" We sucked and chewed on it till we just about fell out of the tree. After that we wiggled and laughed ourselves into some kind of fit. I can still remember how we stayed till it was almost dark and felt dizzy as we helped each other down from the tree house. I threw up four times that day before I got home.

That was one of those good memories, so close to a bad memory, I lowered my head. A slight smile slipped out as I shook my head back and forth. I would never do that again and would never smoke another cigar or cigarette for that matter.

I swung down from the bottom branch onto the soft bed of moss keeping my eyes on the old tree house. Should I go over and straighten out these two boys, I pressed my lips together. They would likely find out the hard way, same as me.

I couldn't help but try to scare them a bit. Very quietly I stepped over to the blind side of the maple. Out of sight I stood under the platform and listened to them.

"Ok I got it going good this time. Here you try it first."

"Wow, this is great. How do you do it?"

"Put it to your lips and suck hard. After that you breathe real deep and take it all down into your lungs."

I stood below the boards gazing at their sneakers with laces dangling and smiled to myself. Once I heard someone sucking in some air, I grabbed one of the feet hanging down. Quick as a whistle the foot was yanked from my grip. I jumped over to the high ground opposite the entry.

Two raggedy boys with pasty faces and unruly hair looked bug eyed in my direction.

I stood with as tough a look as I could muster, squinting my eyes as if studying them. "What are you guys up to? No good I expect."

The boy with the black hair and glasses looked stunned being caught. He had stuffed something into his pocket. His buddy with the wiry red hair reminded me of myself. I looked toward him and bent to pick up the handful of rocks he had discarded.

Running his hand up through his red hair he bent over as he sputtered into a coughing fit. It sounded about like someone being choked trying to get their last breath. Smoke puffed uncontrollably from his mouth. Tears were dripping down his face. Quickly he ran the back of his hand up over his eyes leaving a streak of dirt across his face. No doubt hoping above all odds that no one saw his tears.

The black haired boy started to fidget knowing that his hand inside his pocket was going to have to come out. "Who are you?" With one finger he pushed his glasses up farther on his nose. Suddenly with the cigarette forgotten, his eyes focused on the side of my head with the shaved off hair and the coarse black stitches.

I pointed at his pocket then in slow motion I said, "I... think... I... would... take... that cigarette from your pocket if I were you. It's starting to smoke."

"Gees... holy crap!" He pulled the small red butt out and dropped it to the boards.

The red haired boy continued to cough and choke. Dirty streaks appeared down his face as he stared hard at the nightmare of stitches on the side of my head.

I pulled myself up onto the small platform feeling grown up and tall compared to them. They pulled back as far as they could without leaving the tree, hanging unto the branches opposite the floor. I still held in my hand some of the rocks the wiry haired boy had discarded. Rattling them around in my hand I noticed how smooth and flat they were, great water rocks. I looked at the blank faced boys and said, "Great skippers." I drifted a few in the direction of the same unknown target the other boy had aimed at.

Then I stopped, dropping the rocks to the ground. I tightened my lips around my teeth. I didn't speak for a few more moments. Bending over I picked up the discarded butt. "I would say you boys are too young to be smoking." Putting the butt between my lips I held it tight with my teeth. It was hard not to taste the dryness of a tar residue as the smoke curled up around my eyes, forcing one shut.

The sunny day was turning out real hot. I pulled my jacket off and slung it over my shoulder with the butt held tight between my teeth. Summertime was here and already I had nothing to do. The two boys looked at each other but said nothing.

Uneasiness spread over their faces as they clung to the tree and by now were trying not to look at the gash in the side of my head. This must have been new territory for them both trying to look cool in the face of the unknown.

Removing the butt from my lips I looked hard into their eyes and said, "I should be telling your mama's about this." I rolled the butt between my fingers then returned my gaze to them. "Yes, I know who you are." I replaced the butt between my teeth with my lips spread out.

"I'll be relieving you of this. Take it from me... your mama's won't like it." Bending down I pressed the butt hard into the floor boards destroying all further efforts to smoke it. Grabbing the nearest branch I swung down to the ground and strolled towards home with the feeling of success.

3

CONTROL

I SPUN AROUND ONCE, before I was out of sight from the tree house, for one last look at a piece of my past. Above all odds I hoped the boys listened to me because I really didn't know where they lived. A little bit of fear builds character is what I had always felt.

Somehow my own fear told me I was loosing control with things that mattered in my life. I would have to face mom sooner or later so I headed for home.

When I marched through the door Mom looked up from sweeping the floor and allowed a half smile to spread over her face. I grabbed an apple from the fridge and sat at the kitchen table waiting for her to finish. The crisp apple helped the dry feeling in my mouth left from the cigarette butt.

I poured myself a large glass of cool water and waited. Then she sat down opposite me with the corners of her mouth drooping.

"I'm sorry Mom." I stood up pacing in front of her. "I've no control over my life like I used to have."

"Control, control, that's only an illusion." Mom rubbed cream on her hands as her lips changed into a fine thin line. Pausing for only a moment, she said, "You've never had control."

"I'm older now, I should have more rights."

"You do have rights and I'm listening but I'm sorry Sam. You're at the age now where you need more guidance."

"I'm fourteen past, Mom."

Mom shifted over closer to me. She wrapped her arms around me and squeezed. I could feel the tension build before it crept from my limbs. Tipping my head to one side she inspected the stitches closer.

"I know you're growing up. Problem is you can't possibly know what's completely good for you, not yet. This is where guidance comes in."

I could feel my arms being squashed within her embrace. Her hair brushed the side of my face and still she hugged me hard.

"I love you Sam. This private eye thing… well…I want you safe."

"I love you too Mom, but... but..."

"No buts. You should understand that even seasoned cops get hurt or killed. Age has nothing to do with that. The worry I have for you… well, don't make light of it. It's serious to me."

I tried to push away but her grip was tight. The softness of her hair and the smell of her shampoo made my arms and heart mellow. Within myself I knew she had my best interest at heart.

The week ahead moved very slow as I became aware of the vacant spot left by Connor. I had other friends but somehow I always felt like I was their second choice. The relationship that I shared with Connor had been special. The move in August made me listless. My life was on hold with a vacant summer looming ahead of me. As the time for camp grew closer I had resolved that this was meant to be.

The morning the Acadia bus pulled up, a whole raft of butterflies was released into my stomach. Mom looked red eyed and nervous as she twisted her apron in her hands. Dad arrived and shook my hand while I looked the other way.

"I think you'll like camp." He looked down at his boots and tapped his toes against the side of the step. "I've discussed something else with your mother." Pushing his hands into his pockets he rattled his few coins. I wondered, only wondered if they were the same coins he had rattled a few days before. "In September after you move…I mean if you like…I'll get you your own dog."

I said nothing because I had always wanted a dog. I looked directly into his eyes wondering if this was some kind of bribe. He looked away making no eye contact. Mom had said that life would be different after the move, since all I ever knew was living in an apartment.

Mom grabbed me before I could make any comment. She hugged me hard as the bus ground to a halt and released a burst of air before opening the large door. I could feel her head pushing against the side of my face twisting my glasses at an odd angle. Before I knew it I was being ushered along into the Acadia Lines bus my face still turned toward Dad. I wondered how you could hate someone and still feel guilty. I knew the feelings didn't mix well, somehow it wasn't right.

Two old ladies padded down the isle behind me. I must have been moving too slow because I felt their boney hands push me out of the way. The seats were plush and comfortable. Still unable to smile I waved as Mom's face appeared before me by the edge of the window. Dad stood tall and waved with one single stroke of his hand. I could see Mom's mouth forming the words 'I love you.'

The doors were closed leaving an uneasy feeling over my heart. A lump appeared in my throat pushing against my windpipe the same as it did when I said goodbye to Connor.

I gazed at the outside of the second hand shop with the narrow steps up the side of the building to our apartment. This must have been the first time I really took notice of the building. The weathered siding, shabby as it was suddenly looked so special and felt like an old photograph. It became a snap shot within my mind as I raised my hand and waved with one single stroke at Mom's shiny eyes.

I fought off the tears as I clutched unto a lunch bag mom had pushed into my hand at the last moment. A pain between my shoulders forced me to examine the buildings as I left the only place I had ever called home. Two houses down was Connor's house. My eyes burned as I starred one last time at the new blue siding that was changing his house forever. The small town was neat but nothing special and resembled most places as the bus motored by.

The bus swayed and rolled faster till the whole place was changing into a soft blur in my mind. I twisted back around finding myself trying to think of all the places that I had known. Already I had forgotten important things like the color and the shape of the windows of the main buildings.

The tires on the highway caused a constant hum in my ears. Several times the bus stopped and I continued to watch for familiar faces but saw none. The blank and sometimes pasty looks made no impression on me. The houses were the same as home but felt different and might as well been another country. I thought of Connor and his trip out west. The last time I spoke to him on MSN he seemed so well adjusted. To me he sounded more like a man of the big world.

The sun poured through the windows on my side of the bus. Even though the air was cool I felt as if I had been tightly pressed into a box. The smell of the other bodies suddenly made the air thick. I tried to hold my breath but it did no good.

Then as lunch time approached I could smell someone's sandwich. The air changed as the aroma of onions and smoked meat drifted around me. Dropping the small table on the back of the seat in front of me, I opened my lunch bag. I removed the small juice pack, only slightly cool now. One of my favorite things was three large crumbly chocolate chip cookies in a baggy with an orange twist tie. The homemade bread smelled fresh making me think perhaps everyone could smell just how lucky I had been. I held my favorite sandwich, peanut butter and jam, in my hands and thought of mom. The top slice appeared to slide around on the thick layer of jam. Quickly I took a big bite but chewed real slow.

Missing mom was a new sensation for me. I realized this was the first time we had been apart. A lump formed in my throat once again as I looked at my sandwich.

Random thoughts drifted through my mind while I finished my lunch. Thinking of home stirred resentment deep inside my chest for my father and his part in all this. I had no choice but to go along with things but would hate every minute of it. Hanna Rae had her first job before she was my age plus solved a few mysteries besides. Control had been snatched away by my own father. Gritting my teeth I laid my head back and closed my eyes. Trying hard to clear my mind I soon drifted off to sleep.

"Hey kid… Truro, isn't this your stop?"

I snapped my eyes open and lurched back away from the big nosed man that now shook my shoulder. I grabbed my duffle bag tangled by my feet. "Truro, yes it is."

I understood that I was to wait at the Truro bus station for a man named Brian. This was the first time I realized I should have asked more about the arrangements. People came and went leaving me with an overwhelming feeling of being alone at the end of the world. Just another kid dropped off on the edge of nowhere.

The floor to ceiling windows made for a bright area even with the cloudy sky outside. The only thing of interest was the lineup of vending machines. After I spent my only two dollars

I sat for some time starring at the crispy bars still sparkling in the small windows. Finally I turned to look the other way and sat quietly watching as people hugged and separated. Several buses came and went leaving the large airy station with a stale musty smell adding to my discomfort.

An hour passed and clouds were moving in faster. It looked like rain. Then an old school bus pulled into the parking lot. Large black marks covered what was likely a school name. The bumper hung at an odd angle and the windshield had a large crack across the passenger side. Several kids, with puppy dog eyes, sat hugging bags to their chest gazing out the dusty windows. A stab of sympathy filled me as I felt an odd sense of companionship to more abandoned kids.

A skinny man from the bus rushed inside and moved towards me with such speed I was repulsed. His hair was pulled back into a thin pony tail and his face was covered with a thousand wrinkles. His smile appeared below a wide flat nose, a fighter's nose.

"Sam, Sam O'Brien."

I stood and tried to look casual wondering how he knew me. It likely wasn't hard since I was the only person left waiting for someone.

"My name is Brian Hart. I'm a friend of your dad's from way back."

I figured this was supposed to endear him to me. It didn't work for I felt an instant dislike for his wrinkled smile. I nodded my head as I looked at the bus and shifted my weight to lift the bag up from the floor.

Brian grabbed the bag ripping it from my hands. He continued to talk as he moved away from me. "Sorry I'm late. I had a flat." Reaching the bus door he stepped back, passing me my duffle bag then pushing me in first with his boney fingers pressed into my back. "I've got a couple more stops to make before we head to camp."

The bus smelled of exhaust and dust. I sat about half way back behind some younger kids. The seats were hard and the windows were streaked with dirt. The bus headed away from town leaving me once more with a feeling of no control.

Every time I looked at the other passengers they looked the other way. Didn't they understand I was now one of them? Even though the stitches were gone I knew they likely wondered how I got such a wide gash in the side of my head. Perhaps I should lie and tell everyone that I was a victim of family abuse. Lying never came easy to me so I let the thought slip from my mind. Once more I was drawn to gaze out the streaked windows.

The sign said Onslow as the bus shook and vibrated up the ramp. We turned left crossing over the highway below us. The low flat building had strange long narrow windows facing the road. Central Colchester Jr. High is what the sign read. Rolling the name over in my mind, I was sure that Mom said I would be going there in the fall.

We were almost past the school when the bus jerked sharp right nearly shaking us all from our seats. I took notice of the white knuckled grips on the hands of anyone nearby. Hugging my only belongings I watched as several groups of other shorter kids climbed on. They all appeared to know each other and chattered for some time. I found myself hoping that I wasn't the only taller person in the whole camp.

Then a boy about my age climbed onto the bus. He was heavy set and thicker than normal around the middle. His black hair hung in his eyes as he moved past my seat. He hustled along the dusty floor towards the back seats when one of the little kids yelled, "Hey Mack, you dropped your hat."

The boy spun around and this was the first time that our eyes met. Grabbing his hat out of mid air he flopped down in the nearest seat. Within moments his face was hidden behind a crossword book. Several times I noticed him peaking around the edge of his book gawking at the side of my head. Finally I swiveled around and looked directly at him.

"Hi, my name is Sam, Sam O'Brien."

Mack turned gazing behind him as if I were speaking to someone else. Twisting back facing me he dropped his book down and said, "Your first time for camp?"

"Yea, we're moving to Onslow in the fall. My dad's idea, for camp I mean. Well I guess it's his idea for us to move here to." I lowered my head then grabbed the back of the seat in front of me as the bus lurched ahead at an abnormal speed. "Did he call you Mack?"

"Yea, I'm Mackenzie Lake. Everyone calls me Mack." He paused as he looked out the window. Reaching up he pressed his closed fist to the window and tried to rub the dust off the glass. The grime was on the outside. He shrugged his shoulders before looking back at me then said, "This is my first time at camp too."

4

WILLIE'S ISLAND

EVERYONE'S ATTENTION WAS PULLED back onto the journey. We didn't travel far before the brakes squealed as the bus ground to a halt. The chattering only slowed for a moment. Brian reached over to pull hard on the handle to open the door. It appeared to be broken as he growled under his breath something about a piece of junk. Grabbing hold of the metal post that was attached to the roof he leaned back and kicked the door hard with the flat of his foot.

Everything was silent except for the feelings of rage being vented at the door. I sure hoped this wasn't a sign of how the camp was going to be. After three more kicks to the door, it swung open allowing Brian's face to change back to a normal color, whatever that was. He turned and smiled at us but made no effort to condone or explain his actions.

I looked towards Mack and found that he had returned to his puzzle book. I spoke louder so he could hear me above the chatter of everyone else. "Have you just moved here too?"

Mack raised his eye brows. Once more dropping his book to his lap and for some reason I felt like I was bothering him.

"No, I've always lived in Great Village." He looked out the window then back at me before saying, "About half an hour from here." He resumed looking at his book.

I tried to sound interested as I asked, "How come this is your first time going to camp?"

This time when he dropped his book I could hear the agitation in his voice. "I've three other brothers and I wanted some time to myself." Mack twisted in the seat as he watched other people climb onto the bus.

Time to himself was likely meant as a clue to me. I let things slide with Mack as I watched a batch of young girls, giggle their way down the isle. Three girls a bit younger than me squeezed into the seat behind me. They continued with a nervous whisper as their eyes likely caught sight of my scar.

The last person that climbed onto the bus walked with a swagger down the center of the bus. He was tall and lean with a long nose, or perhaps it was the way he held it up higher. His hair was a silky blond, spiked up in the top allowing the rest to fall like a curtain over his blue eyes. He pulled his shoulders back as he curled his lip up and appeared to be trying hard not to look my way.

He scuffed his sneakers along the gritty floor down the narrow isle towards the back seats. Mack was sitting in the last seat of the left side. The right side was empty but still he stood starring at Mack, who was hidden behind his book.

Then he kicked Mack's sneaker. "Get out of my seat." Mack stood for a moment starring intently into the blue eyes before him. The tall boy stood firm and made no motion to waver in his demand appearing very pleased with his efforts to get a rise out of someone.

Brian spoke in a loud voice from the front of the bus. "Hunter, sit down and shut up. I want no fights."

Hunter swiveled around to face Brian before saying, "Who do you think you are?"

Brian stepped away from the door controls towards Hunter. "Your father doesn't own this bus yet."

Hunter looked around at the shabby battered seats and said, "Why would my father want to own a piece of junk like this?"

Mack gathered himself up and moved to a seat a few rows closer to me. Hunter took his seat and started to give the rest of the occupants the once over.

Brian returned to his controls and said in a loud voice, "We'll be at the camp within the next half hour."

He pulled the bus back onto the road. The rain started to pound down hard. The sound of the rain on the roof muffled the roaring sound of the engine. The whomp, whomp of the wipers became a repetitive normal rhythm. Then one wiper stopped working properly, skipping over the windshield like fingernails on a chalkboard, then stopped completely.

The stranded wiper allowed the rain to blur my vision out the passenger's side of the windshield. The houses along the road soon gave way to trees on each side of the bus. No control over my destiny once more gave me an uneasy feeling. The dark clouds pressed the sky down closer to the road and bus. Gradually the motor slowed down and the road became more twisty and bumpy.

The rain drummed down even harder before Brian finally pulled the bus to a halt. Everyone looked at the doorway now opened, without another incident. There was no greeting except a muddy yard outside. The big lodge stood not more than twenty feet away. He said, "We're the last bus and kind of late."

I lurched up from my seat starting to move towards the door. Hunter grabbed my shoulder shoving me back into my seat. The unspoken rule of everyone following him caught me off guard. I starred at the back of his head but said nothing.

By the time I gathered myself back up, I noticed Mack waiting for me to go ahead of him. Then he said in a low voice just behind my shoulder. "My cousin Jack went to this camp last year. He told me all about Hunter. His father owns all the land around the camp. There's one thing I know for sure, he's big on himself."

I was glad Mack spoke to me, I wasn't alone after all. I pressed my lips together and shook my head. Standing in the bus doorway I gazed around to see two other buses stopped and already empty. The rain had slowed down and it was almost dark making the brightness of the lodge stand out. The enormous log building stood in the middle of the clearing surrounded by forest. I hugged my duffle bag closer to my chest and made the sprint for the lodge.

Once inside I had an instant feeling of being at home. The air smelled of pizza and I knew I would love the food. We were all ushered into the main room. It was brightly lit with large wagon wheel lights hanging from the ceiling. The log walls had a brilliant yellow, varnished look. The room was filled with extra large wooden picnic tables.

A tall thin woman with a weathered face spoke in a loud voice. "Sit wherever you like. I'm sure it's been a long day for some of you. I see we have some regulars but I do see a lot of new faces." She spread her arms out to the sides and said, "Enjoy…I'll speak more after you eat."

While I followed one of the gigglers to the line for a drink, I gazed around. There was no ceiling only dark stained wooden rafters. Hooked to the wood above our heads were at least a hundred paddles. Each one had a name burned into the wood. Some paddles had pictures painted on them and others were tacked to the walls with blocky letters listing the rules. I noticed each line started with a capital NO.

I took a bite of the largest piece of pepperoni pizza. That's when I noticed it, in the corner of the room at the end of a long line of windows stood a giant wooden Mi'kmaq Chief. It was nothing short of amazing.

Mack leaned towards me and said, "My cousin told me, he's carved out of one single piece of wood with a chainsaw."

Before long the tall woman stood before the tables and spoke in a loud deep voice. "I guess everyone is here now. I would like to get everyone settled before it gets too dark. Welcome to the big lodge of 'Willie's Summer Camp'. My name is Sadie. Each team will have there own counselor, but all counselors wear a red top and are willing to help anyone. This camp has been operating since 1968. It's taken a long time but through the years we've built quite a following."

Sadie's eyes ran over the large group of campers before proceeding. "The camp is divided into four teams called Angry Coyote, Running Bear, Lone Wolf, and Soaring Eagle."

Suddenly there was an increase in the level of noise. I looked around and wondered at the same time how they picked the people for each group. Whispering to myself I prayed for the luck of the Irish to be with me because I didn't want Hunter in my group.

Sadie raised her hands and spoke even louder. "I would like everyone to line up in front of the tables. We'll pick the teams right now then I'll give each one a key to a locker in the cabins."

She pointed her long finger towards two girls and said, "I want the tallest for captains and now two boys. To be on the fair side each team has to have an equal number of boys and girls."

As luck would have it, I was one of the tallest boys in the whole camp.

"I would like each of you to step forward and tell us your name. Pull a team name from this bag. Then we'll start picking your teams."

"My name is Dee Webb and my teams name is Soaring Eagle."

"My name if Hunter Stead and my teams name is Lone Wolf."

"My name is Debbie Baker and my teams name is Running Bear."

"My name is Sam O'Brien and my teams name is Angry Coyote."

Everyone cheered and then went silent waiting for someone to pick them. The process went slow. The only person I knew was Mack. He looked pleased to be my first choice or perhaps it was nothing more than not being on Hunter's team.

I noticed one girl with a very dramatic look. At once I knew she would be my first choice of the girls. Hunter had picked mostly the biggest of the group and soon looked uninterested in the whole process.

Each person said their name out loud as they were chosen. The first girl I chose was Nyla Timble. I figured she would be about thirteen wrapped in a tough exterior. Her hair was cut to a brush cut except for a couple inches at the top of her head. The long hair was dyed purple and hung down almost to her shoulders over the brown stubble. From beneath the long purple hair I noticed three earrings on only one ear.

She marched towards me and as she drew closer my eyes were drawn to a small purple star tattooed on the edge of her neck line. Her brilliant green eyes didn't waver as she looked directly at me. She reached up and tugged at her earrings, only slightly. I was pleased with my choice.

Sadie proceeded to point to the map that stood on a large easel by the far edge of the room. The map showed every area at the camp plus the cabins for the teams. The four cabins on the right were for the guys and the other four on the left were for the girls.

Everyone moved in line behind the leader of each team. The rain outside had stopped and the sun was long gone leaving nothing more than a damp woody smell. Behind the big lodge were eight log cabins each with its own sign above the door. The girls from my team moved on towards their cabin as

I stood there watching the moon light shimmer over the still water of the lake.

In the darkness I could see a large island some distance from the shoreline. Tall trees loomed over the edge of the water closest to me. I could hear the bumping of the canoes tied to a wharf. I wondered for the first time what my mom would be doing tonight. I felt my stomach twist with the feeling of being so far away from home. Then a quick flare of anger made my stare freeze. Home, ha that wasn't really my home anymore now was it.

My thoughts came back to the here and now as I looked behind me. Mack stood looking at the island as he hugged his satchel to his chest. His face looked blank, pasty and lost. We both at the same time looked down and turned towards the cabins.

"It's called Willie's Island. Do you suppose anyone lives there?"

Before I could answer I noticed a huddle of girls about fifteen feet away. There was no mistake I could tell even from this distance that Hunter was talking to them. One of the girls that stood out was an Angry Coyote. I wasn't sure how much responsibility came with being a captain. My attention turned to what Hunter was now saying.

Hunter stood tall gazing at someone. "My, don't we like ourselves?" He moved around the group singling out one girl, it was Nyla. "I could like this. The summer has just exploded with new possibilities. What was your name again...Twyla?"

5

CAPTAIN SAM

I STROLLED TOWARDS THE group then paused. Thinking to myself I wondered, what a captain's duties were. When I raised my head, I saw Mack's plump shape march past me, moving towards the group.

"My name is Nyla and I don't care what you like or don't like." She tried to step around Hunter. He stepped in front of her once more. She placed her hands on her hips and tipped her head sideways. Dropping her hands to her side she reached up and tugged at her earring.

"I was just trying to be nice." Hunter had a smirk on his face as he got a good look at her hair. "What a mess. Where did you come up with this idea?"

Nyla stood still looking him directly in the face. Her body actions became more rigid as her arms hung straight, her hand clutched to her satchel. In a stern voice I could hear her say, "Get out of my way."

"Oh, feisty are we?" Hunter gazed at her then a smile lit up his face.

Mack dropped his bag and stepped between Hunter and Nyla. He glared towards Hunter as he pulled his shoulders back square. Pausing he clenched his fists to his sides and spoke in a loud voice, "She said …get out of her way."

It only took seconds to know I was going to be drawn into this. My hands still gripped tight to my duffle bag as I moved in closer.

Nyla reached up and spun Mack around to face her. "I can fight my own battles."

Disbelief registered on Mack's plump face. "You're an Angry Coyote and we stick together. Don't forget you're part of a team now."

Nyla rolled her eyes and said, "Whatever, come on Lacey lets leave the boys to their little games." The two girls turned and walked towards their cabin.

Hunter reached over and grabbed the front of Mack's t-shirt pulling him off balance. "This is none of your business little Mack." Hunter looked down over Mack's ample belly then he laughed as he said, "Don't get your buns in a twist, Big Mack. I was only trying to get to know little Miss Nyla." Hunter turned towards his hefty followers and snickered.

I stepped closer to Hunter and pulled his hand from the front of Mack's t-shirt. My eyes burned as I starred directly at Hunter, daring him to do anything at all. Within seconds, Hunters face became redder than what I thought would be humanly possible. Once I had detached Hunter's hand from Mack I was flying by the seat of my pants. An odd feeling deep down told me I was meant to be their captain and with that came an unspoken kind of loyalty.

The flash of a bright red shirt came out of nowhere and sure enough standing beside me was Sadie. Her voice was very harsh as she said, "Hunter… move it. I want no trouble here." She didn't look at Mack or myself but spoke to Hunter only. "Don't make me sorry I made you a captain."

"I didn't ask for it."

"Your father would like you to grow up a bit this year maybe even show us all you can be more responsible." Sadie didn't waver in her focus.

Sadie and Hunter were deep in discussion as I took hold of Mack by the shoulder pushing his duffle bag into his hands. Then I aimed him towards the cabin with the sign above the door that read Angry Coyote.

In a low voice I whispered, "Forget him, he's not worth it. Besides, did you see his two big goons standing behind him? I think their names are Hink and Dink. I figure he picked them just for scenes like this."

Mack twisted back around to see Nyla walking away. Then he said, "What he did to me on the bus, well I'm still peeved." After a few more steps he laughed under his breath and asked, "Their names aren't really Hink and Dink are they?"

I lifted my shoulders in a shallow shrug as we moved closer to our cabin. I opened the door and noticed a slow creaking sound. The dark interior came with a strange damp, all consuming feeling.

My fingers fumbled over the switch by the door. The single light on the ceiling flickered sending a dim light into the corners of the small area. The beds were lined up against one side to the left of the door. The opposite wall had several small windows, plain wooden frames with loose glass slightly rattling in the breeze. Under the windows there was a small table and several wooden benches up against the wall.

The younger boys Jacob and Carter pushed past me as they made the quick choice of which bed they wanted. I turned and looked towards Dakota, the youngest of my choices, a shy boy with long dark hair. He was nine or perhaps a small ten and came across as a first year camper for sure. Hugging his tattered bag close to his chest Dakota looked directly at me for the first time. His dark brown eyes were filled with tears as his gaze shifted to the side of my head. The scar and the nightmare it offered starred back at him. Holding his lip tight between his teeth he said nothing, only starred.

"You can have the middle bed Dakota. I'll stand guard in the closest bed to the door." A sign of relieve spread over his face.

Dakota moved quickly towards his bed as if he didn't want to take any chances. Mack flung his bag on the bed next to mine. I dropped my duffle bag and stood looking over what was to be my home for the next six weeks. The small flat beds were close to the floor each with a new sleeping bag placed on top of a flattened pillow.

On the far wall opposite the door were five old dented lockers. The fronts had several rows of old ninja turtle stickers scattered over them. The interior of the cabin had nothing covering the studs. A few old Nintendo posters, one of Zelda and another of Mario, were tacked to the walls. The paper was curled on the corners and weathered from years of finger prints. Every here and there was a knot hole missing just the size for spying through.

Mack sat down on his bed as he gazed around. He was the first to comment as he cleared his throat. "Oh, real warm and inviting."

I looked around the room then at the cob webs in the corners of the windows. Pulling my locker key from my pocket I dropped it on the table. Turning around I looked towards the boys and said, "I'm your captain and this is home boys, at least for the next six weeks. We should all try to get along and stick together, look out for each other. It's not a hotel, its camp."

I explained my war wound on the side of my head which answered most of the questions they likely had. It could have been my imagination but I believe they all felt better after we talked a while.

The rain once more started drumming on the roof and mixing with the breeze. It had been a long day but finally we crawled into our sleeping bags. I reached over and turned the light out. Flopping back into the dampness of the bed I gazed above at the ceiling of the camp. The breeze outside whistled through the holes in the walls. The scraping of a branch across the glass every now and then didn't make it any easier to sleep.

After only a few minutes Dakota asked in a low whisper, "Captain Sam, what's that noise?"

"It's a branch outside scrapping against the window glass. Don't worry I'll fix it tomorrow. You're Ok, I'll be right here, you're not alone."

In a lower voice he asked, "Captain Sam, can I keep my flashlight on."

"Sure you can, Dakota."

Dakota clicked his flashlight on and said nothing more. I watched as the faded beam of light flicked up over the roof and reflected off the windows. The outside light from the lodge dappled the walls with the shadows from the trees. The last thing I remembered was the flashlight being focused on a spider working hard at the corner of the window frame. Finally I dropped off to sleep despite the wind howling around the edge of the door and the constant scraping from the branch.

Before I even opened my eyes the next morning I was awe struck with the silence that engulfed me. The rain had stopped and the breeze was only slight as the poplar leaves rattled outside. I opened my eyes immediately noticing the bright sunshine that was blazing in above my head.

I snuggled down into the comfort of my sleeping bag and closed my eyes once more. Then I noticed a soft sound of two feet padding their way over to my bedside. When I opened my eyes not more than a foot away was Dakota's black eyes starring directly into my face.

"Captain Sam, do I have to stay in bed like at home?"

"No, I suppose not." I closed my eyes and breathed deep. Then I could feel his breath on my face. I decided to let on I had gone back to sleep. Moments passed and then he whispered in my ear.

"My Mom tries that too." He didn't speak allowing a few more moments of silence. "Your head looks real sore." All I could hear was his breath whizzing in and out of his stuffed up nose. "Can I go to the big lodge and use the bathroom?"

"Yea."

He rushed back to his bed. The zipping of his bag continued for a bit then he left the cabin. The door didn't latch allowing the breeze to push it open. My eyes were drawn to the doorway and I knew there would be no more sleep for me. Rolling over I noticed once more my jeans lying on the top of a hump of clothing. Pulling my clothes on I stood by the edge of the doorway.

The lake was beyond the centre and looked very inviting. The slight breeze was mixed with the rattling of the poplar leaves and the sounds of the morning chickadee's. There wasn't much movement around but I did notice two men standing by a back door at the big lodge.

The short man had a white apron wrapped around his waist and held a death grip on a large steel spoon. He was shaking the spoon at a younger man. The same younger man was wearing a red counselor shirt and was swinging his arms around in a frustrated manner. As I made my way towards the excitement, the counselor, catching site of me, rushed around the corner of the building out of site.

The cook swiveled around to face me. His face was mostly nose and rough with stiff starchy white whiskers. "What?" He coughed but clearing his throat didn't improve the raspy sound. Not even waiting for my response he continued with more of his gruffness.

"Stay out of my way, use the other door around front."

I stepped back away from the man wondering, who hired him. Around the corner, there was a gaggle of kids standing on the edge of a rocky beach that was about twenty feet wide. The water on the lake sparkled with a mirror effect. The same tall counselor pushed his way into the middle of the kids. I stood back away from the group, listening.

"My name is John and after breakfast Sadie will outline the start up of camp."

One skinny boy with binoculars to his face pointed with a long lean finger towards the island that loomed in the distance. "Look out there, I see a boat over by the far side of that island."

John swiveled in the direction the boy was pointing to. His head moved back and forth scanning the shadows along the edge of Willie's island. Twisting around to his left, he counted the canoes all still tied in place.

The skinny boy stepped closer to John and said, "Does anyone live on that island?"

"No, no one has lived there for years. It must have been a shadow."

"I know a shadow when I see one. I say there's someone living over there. When do we go to explore that place?"

I walked over to the far right of the beach, closer to the waters edge and stood gazing towards the dark shadows under the island trees that loomed in the distance. Nothing appeared to be moving that I could see.

The water below where I stood was dark and showed a deepness that I imagined would be a great swimming hole. To my right was a large branched pine with a rope hanging straight down. At the base of the rope was a large knot. A good place to swing over the water and drop into the deepest spot.

John raised his voice so all that were listening could hear. "The island is off limits. We have lots of area here to explore." With that he raised his arms and spoke in a commanding voice, "It's time for breakfast, everyone inside now."

Then I noticed a fish jump creating circles in the still water. I was starting to get hungry and for the first time I looked forward to exploring the camp. Perhaps it was going to be more interesting than I had imagined.

"Captain Sam, did you see that fish?"

Dakota was standing beside me. I nodded my head and turned towards the lodge. He looked directly at me and for the first time I could see curiosity in his face.

"My uncle Tom used to hunt and fish on the island many years ago. He says the place is haunted by a ghost named Willie." Dakota cleared his throat as he looked me in the face.

I paused and spoke with a captain's authority saying, "Did you hear John, Dakota? It's off limits. Besides, there's no such thing as ghosts."

6

SCAVENGER HUNT

WHEN I FOLLOWED THE others inside I realized there were more people up than I thought. The smell of pancakes and syrup made me feel hungry. Before long, all my Coyotes were eating along side of me.

Sadie started to fill in some of the blanks. The captains were sort of in charge of their teams but each member would be just as powerful when it came to right and wrong.

Sadie said, "We have tons of programs and there will be lots of freedom for each person to pick something of interest. Some are group orientated activities and others are for different age levels. To start with we have a scavenger hunt planned."

Each team was given a map likely to get us all familiar with the layout of the camp. We were told at the end of the trail, marked with an X, we would find a parcel containing a list of items we would have to find on the return. There are ten people to each team all ranging from 9 to 14. There would be a badge of honor given to the most impressive find plus the first team back with all the items would get to pick the next activity.

Our map circled the area around the sawdust pile. I directed everyone to follow me and stay close. A light breeze coupled with the hot sun pressed the feeling of fresh air deep into my soul.

Leaving the lodge we headed to the left. We passed an area that had large rocks around blackened bonfire pits.

Carter rushed ahead of me as he pointed to a basketball pad and hoop. "This is going to be fun. Last year my group won the first game." His face brightened only to then look glum as he said, "But we came in third in the finals."

The group was traveling along pretty good when we came to a pine grove. I stopped and thought for the first time today of Connor.

Mack stood and looked up the trees then said, "I can't climb trees real good." He hung his head and kicked the dirt with the toe of his sneaker.

Nyla and Lacey stopped beside him. Nyla looked up the side of the tree. She pulled at her earrings then said, "That's ok. I'm afraid of heights so I'll stay on the ground with you."

Mack looked towards her and smiled after looking away.

The area was wooded and I noticed on the map there were a few smaller islands to the right. We traveled along a smooth sandy path until we noticed the lake once more. There, not far from shore, were two jagged islands. The smooth path ended at the edge of the water which looked shallow for some distance.

Dakota looked up towards me and said, "My uncle Tom told me the islands are called the Stepping Stone Islands."

"You're right, that's what the map says also." I folded the map once more and said, "Well I imagine, John meant all the islands are off limits." I looked towards Dakota to be sure he understood me.

We traveled along side the edge of the lake in good view of the smaller islands until we came to a brook that fed into the lake. Some of the boys ran and jumped the brook. A few of the girls and Dakota got soaked.

"According to the map this is Galloping Brook and that over there is called the Big Rock." I looked at the Coyotes before asking, "What do you say lets see what's on the other side of that big wall of rock?"

Nyla stood looking up the side of the rock and said, "It looks pretty high to me. Is the X on the other side? I mean, do we have to go that far?"

Mack paused then spoke up, "What can it hurt Nyla? They can climb up over the big rock if they want. We'll walk around it and meet them on the other side."

Nyla reached up and tugged at one of her earrings, then looked at Mack before she said, "Yea, Ok then."

We split up into two groups to meet on the other side. The rock protruding from the earth with its rounded edges was making it easy to climb. At the top of the rock was a great view.

In the distance I could tell we had walked almost all the way around to the other side of the lake. This side of Willie's Island was hidden from the camp. I noticed a pile of metal barrels with the rusty edges protruding from tall brown grass and surrounded by leafless bushes. From where I stood, I could see a sandbar that connected the island to the mainland.

As I was gazing around from high on top of the rock, Dakota pointed towards the far edge of the sandbar. "Look over there, I see a red shirt. It must be one of the counselors."

Sure enough I saw the tall red shape before it slipped out of sight.

Dakota looked towards me with his eye brows bunched up. "How come, if it's off limits, he's over there?"

"Never mind Dakota, perhaps they are checking for the boat someone thought they saw there earlier."

We climbed down on the other side of the rock to rejoin our group. Before long we found our package sitting on top of a tree stump. The items to collect on the return were mostly in the open. We all had a blast exploring the area. It didn't appear to bother anyone that we were the last team to get back to the camp.

The badge of honor was given to the most impressive item found. Dakota won the prize, hands down, for an eagle feather. Even though our team lost, Dakota was beaming with the badge of honor. The winning team chose to have tug of war games and swimming challenges next.

The days that followed were filled with many challenges. The sunny days and evening campfires pulled our teams together. I found myself feeling like we were all more than campers. Even though I was the captain, my fellow Angry Coyotes watched out for me too as we began to feel more like a family.

Sometime during the first week we were divided into teams for a canoe challenge. I was very pleased to have Mack and Nyla on my team. I was in charge of steering the canoe while Mack put some muscle into the speed. Nyla was quick on her feet and was a natural choice to be our runner.

We were to have many challenges and different trials. At the last week of camp there was to be a final race for a championship. There will be several check points around the camp area and once the canoe reached a certain point then the runner will jump from the boat and race to a set point and complete a task to collect an item before returning to the boat, where we will be waiting. This challenge was the most important thing of the summer. Beating the Lone Wolf's team and Hunter was on all our minds. After the basic lesson on life vests, water safety and maneuvering a canoe we spent many hours practicing.

Every day the three of us found time to practice for the canoe challenge. One afternoon during our practice time I stopped paddling. I looked towards the camp and the races that were taking place with the younger kids. The distant yelling and cheering made me smile. I paused as I laid the paddle across the edge of the boat then said, "You know, somewhere inside my mind I understand my father was trying to help by sending me to camp."

Nyla said, "It would be nice to have a father that cared enough to do that."

I thought for a moment then said, "I didn't like the fact I had been sent away but all in all the camp experience has been pretty good."

Mack turned slightly to look back, and then said. "Yea, my father works all the time so it's like I have one but don't have one. In my case I was the one that wanted to get away."

I focused on the water dripping off my paddle. I noticed Nyla looking over the edge of the boat, dipping her fingers into the water every now and then.

Mack looked towards the big island and said, "Well camp, I mean time away, seems to make me think more. I should be glad for my family. Mom seems so frantic most of the time."

I watched as Nyla continued to move her fingers in circles now but she said nothing, only listened.

I realized that the three of us had many things in common as far as families went. I said, "My mom had it hard for a bunch of years. It was a good thing for me having JC around. He filled the father gap for most things."

Mack turned and frowned towards me "My older brother wasn't concerned about me or anyone but himself."

I looked towards Mack now and said, "You almost sound jealous of him."

Mack shrugged his shoulders and dipped his paddle back into the water. "I felt angry more than anything, but I always had my grandfather. Even the twins Brad and Chad never bothered much with him. They were too young to go fishing and that's where we went most of the time."

Nyla pulled her hand out of the water now and gazed towards the camp after a sudden burst of yelling from the swing by the swimming hole. "You guys don't know how good you got it with sisters and brothers, even Grandfathers. I never had anyone but my grandmother Helen. She never cared for kids and sure didn't take much to me."

Mack removed his hat and ran his hand up over his forehead. Twisting the hat back onto his head he started to paddle some more before saying, "My Grandfather has been dead now for must be six months."

Nyla reached forward and placed her hand on Mack's shoulder and said, "Sorry. You must really miss him. I feel like I've always missed the family I never had."

I gripped my paddle once more and dropped it back into the water twisting the handle to steer us towards the far side of the lake.

Nyla spoke very slowly as she dropped her hand back into the water creating ripples as the boat moved forward. "I suppose Mom sending me to camp was a good thing. Being an only child and never knowing my father wasn't real easy. After the tattoo and hair cut Mom decided to send me off to camp, something about too much time with the wrong crowd. I cried and screamed loads but she wouldn't have any of it. Her mind was made up by then. Sometimes I feel like my whole life has been shaped by the absence of a father."

Then I thought for a moment and said, "Maybe you should think more about the best thing you have."

Nyla twisted and looked towards me with her fingers playing with her earrings before asking, "What do ya mean?"

"I mean perhaps you should be grateful for the mother you have and that she cares."

We continued to get closer to the island. My mind drifted away from the family talk and I began to tell them about the cook, Charlie Chip and John arguing the first morning here.

Nyla spoke up as she turned to look back at the camp. "I heard Charlie was a fill in for someone that quit camp before it started. He's always angry and I've seen him sneaking around some distance from the kitchen. He gives me the creeps most of the time."

Mack laughed and then said, "I think he just looks rough with those whiskers all over his face. I hope my whiskers are the soft kind like my Grandfathers."

Nyla laughed and pushed on Mack's back. "I think you have a while before you have to worry about whiskers."

We all laughed and even Mack grunted in response to her comments.

"It seems odd being told to stay away from the island." I stopped paddling again and look at the blue sky. "There was a mystery hanging around this island. Besides I don't know what Charlie and John would have to argue about so early in the camping season."

Nyla said, "John is a first year counselor but I don't think he's very good at the camping thing. Sometimes I feel like he wants to be anywhere but here."

The mystery of the island lay silent in the back of my mind for days till we were given the map for the final race. After supper we decided to paddle over towards Willie's Island and see if we could find a short cut over the sandbar towards the end mark of the final race. After we reached the first stopping point Nyla jumped from the boat and started off at a good pace towards the first marker.

We waited for some time for her to return. When she arrived back at the waters edge she was pale and out of breath.

I said, "What took so long?"

"I stumbled when I noticed someone on the edge of the hill. I stepped behind a tree and watched. It looked like Charlie Chip and he was dragging something in a large bag, it looked heavy."

I looked towards Mack as his mouth dropped open. "There's something strange about him. He's just not right."

I felt like he was reading my mind. "This morning Dakota told me he went to the bathroom late last night and he heard that Charlie Chip and John arguing again."

Mack and Nyla were both staring at me now. Nyla twisted back around in the canoe as she said, "What about?"

"Dakota said it sounded like John was telling Charlie to stay away from the boats. It didn't make much sense to Dakota and when they noticed him they both stopped talking right away."

Nyla rolled her eyes and said, "Not everyone gets along you know. It simply doesn't mean there's something bad going on."

Mack gripped the handle of the paddle and twisted around to look at Nyla. "Well what's with the bag Charlie was trying to hide then?"

Nyla scrunched her face up, wrinkling her nose as she looked up at the sky, "Maybe it was supper?"

We all laughed once more but I had a sick feeling in my stomach. I pointed towards the shadowed side of Willie's Island. "Let's paddle over toward that point. If you're right Mack and there's a way around the island then it could give us an edge over Hunter in the challenge."

We went quite a distance without saying a word. The sun blistered out from behind the clouds that had floated around all day. My vest was tied too tight making beads of sweat pop out on my forehead. The water had a dark mirrored effect then just as suddenly a stretch of long watery weed reaching for the bottom of our boat. Once around the bend we were out of sight of the main part of camp.

In the distance there was the sandbar that I had noticed before. I twisted the edge of my paddle to point the boat towards the fast approaching sandbar.

Nyla's voice was low as she turned to look toward me. "We're not going on the island, are we?"

I found myself being drawn into the mystery of the island. The tall dark spruce trees shadowed everything with an ancient deserted feeling. Then I took notice of Nyla's hands with a white knuckle grip on the edge of the canoe. "No Nyla, we're not allowed. My insides twisted with those words leaving a residue of a bad feeling deep inside. I hated those words, you're not allowed."

Mack rested his paddle on the edge of the canoe as we coasted. The silence was complete. My attention was drawn to the sound of the water dripping off his paddle into the lake. I twisted my handle once more bringing us to a halt.

"What's that? I see something in behind that clump of trees. Over there to the left." I watched the back of his head twist back and forth searching before I said, "Beyond that big maple, farther to the right, do you see it Mack?"

Nyla shaded her eyes with her hand but was silent as she searched the area for the clues from my directions.

We pushed farther on and when we rounded the bend there before our eyes was a large weathered house, practically hidden with overgrown bushes. Some of the windows were nothing more than holes in the walls, black and spooky. An old balcony hung onto the front of the house with the other side of the house falling down unto the remnants of an old brick flue.

Silently our canoe glided closer till the bottom ground to a halt touching the gritty rocks still pointing towards the sand bar. From this angle there looked to be a path where the weeds were patted down leading towards the house. Even from here I could see deep ruts on the sandbar.

"No, Nyla we're not going on the island." Pointing towards the sandbar, I said, "Look over there Mack. We could push the canoe over the sandy area and we would have access to the water on the other side."

While we were looking at the sandbar, out of nowhere came John up behind us in his canoe. "What are you guys doing over here? Stop right there, you know this is off limits. Turn that boat around and head back, right now. This is out of bounds."

7

AFTER DARK

I TURNED TO LOOK John in the face as I felt a heat crawl up the back of my neck. I burst out, blurring my words together. "We're looking for a quicker route for the final canoe challenge."

John pointed back towards the camp and said in a deep stern voice, "The camp is that way." His voice rose higher as his finger stretched towards the camp back in the distance. "I don't ever want to see you over here again. Get a move on."

I quickly steered the boat around as Mack started paddling. Nyla sat very still, her back poker straight and her legs neatly tucked beneath her. Her hands gripped to the sides of the canoe. Only the sound of the paddles slapping the water broke the uncomfortable silence. I expected John was following us. Before we rounded the bend I glanced back finding John and his canoe nowhere in sight.

The sun was completely gone by the time we arrived back at the dock lined with the other canoes. Nyla climbed out of the boat and only then did she realize that John wasn't with us. "Where's John!"

Mack stood looking at the far edge of Willie's Island. "I can't see him. Where do you suppose he went?"

Clouds were splattered across the red sky. Sadie stood on the step of the main lodge with her hands on her hips. She starred towards us and then raised her hand over her eyes as if to stare beyond us towards the island shadows in the distance. For some time she said nothing then she raised her voice. "The bonfires will be on tonight. I want everyone to gather an arm-load of firewood from the pile behind the basketball area."

Nyla yelled, "Lacey." She waved her arm frantically then turned to speak to us. "I'll see you guys at the bonfire."

Mack and I headed past the bonfire pits, to the right of the lodge. A large gaggle of kids were starting to gather around the wood pile. To one side of the wood pile stood Hunter with his arms folded neatly across his chest.

He watched as Hink and Dink loaded each other with large pieces of wood. Once he noticed me he glared at us with an icy stare. "Did John find you guys?"

Mack instantly puffed his chest up and stepped towards Hunter. "What do you mean? How did you know?"

"Well, did you think John found you by accident?" he belched out a stupid sounding laugh and looked toward his buddies. Right on cue they started to grunt out another sound almost foreign to the human ear. "You guys are in deep trouble going near that island. And you Sam! What a captain, ha? You'll likely be the first captain in the history of summer camp to be kicked out."

I stared at Hunter with a burning feeling inside as I clenched my fists. I think he hated to see how close our team had become. He was constantly commenting on my ability to set a good example. I had a hard time to resist getting into a match of wits with him.

"You're supposed to be the captain and lead your team. You did a good job leading them into trouble. Your height was the only reason you got the job. There was no consideration for brains." We stood eye to eye and he still managed to look down his long nose at me.

My mind was full of some pretty mean things to sling at Hunter. My lips felt like they were on fire as I looked down and there watching my every move was Dakota, Carter and Jacob. I don't really know where all the strength came from but somehow I twisted around and walked away.

Mack caught up with me. Taking his hat off and twisting it around in his hands he turned to watch the side of my head. "I can't believe you walked away from that. I thought you had more spunk in ya."

He stopped and turned around heading back towards the wood pile. I watched him and wondered what to say; before I knew it he was out of range. I had to agree with Mack. Why did I stop? I felt ashamed that I wasn't able to look more powerful than Hunter. From where I stood I could see Dakota, Carter and Jacob still standing close to Hunter's group.

I stood looking towards the rest of the campers. I didn't feel like taking part any longer. As Sadie walked past me towards the camp fires, I stopped her.

"Sadie, I'm feeling really tired. Could I skip the bonfires tonight? I want to go to my cabin if I could, please."

Her hand shot up to my forehead and concern filled her face. "Are you sick?"

"No, no. I'm fine. I'm just not in the mood for any company tonight."

"OK, if you're sure."

I nodded and turned towards the cabin. Once I reached the cabin I looked back to the area now full of kids and counselors. To one side I could see Mack sitting with Nyla and Lacey. I looked down at the weathered step and sat for awhile. The sky was sparkling with millions of diamond specks. The air was filled with normal night noises of the forest behind the cabins. In the distance I could hear the laughter of the campers as one of the counselors told a nightmare of a story.

I gathered myself up from the step and entered the peaceful darkness of the cabin. Prying my feet from my sneakers, I dropped my jeans on top the pile. Climbing into my sleeping bag, I was off to sleep faster than I could have imagined. It was late before the rest of my Coyotes turned in for the night. I lay there in a sleepy stupor and never let on I was awake. Dakota was asking Mack if he was second captain when I wasn't there.

Mack sounded impatient as he answered, "No Dakota. Now go to bed and be quiet or you'll wake Sam."

I lay there for some time rolling thoughts over and over in my head. It seemed odd to me that Sadie said nothing about the island or us being caught. When the air was filled with the heavy sounds of sleep I looked at my watch tipping it towards the moonlight that was coming through the windows. It was 3:45. I had to use the bathroom. Very quietly I pulled my jeans on and stepped out the door.

The moon was bright casting shadows over the front of the cabins. I stood outside the doorway scanning the yard towards the lodge while I soaked up the peace. Deep inside I was glad I had been sent to camp even though I wouldn't want to admit that to my father. The call of a loon broke the silence. I watched the moonlight flutter among the clouds making the lake sparkle like black gems. In this short time I had developed a love for the outdoors and a camper's life. Everything was quiet and soaked in a darkened haze as I headed for the washroom in the main lodge.

Afterwards when I came out of the side door of the lodge I noticed someone down by the edge of the lake. Watching from the shadows I could see someone tie up a canoe. It was John's tall lanky shape.

Within moments I could see someone else leaning against a tree not far from my own. The chunky shape moved with some speed grabbing John's shoulder. I wasn't close enough to make out what was being said. It sounded like Charlie Chip's gruff voice. I tried to move closer without being noticed.

Charlie grunted, "Where've you been?"

John jumped raising his hands in a boxer style. "Oh it's you. I didn't think anyone would still be up."

"That doesn't answer my question. Where were you?"

John said, "I don't think it's any concern of yours."

Charlie stepped in front of John blocking his path. "I'm going to make it my concern."

John starred straight into Charlie's face. "Last time I checked, you were a cook."

Then John walked around Charlie heading for the counselor quarters. Charlie grabbed John's shoulder and pulled him back around to face him.

John was surprised but still very quick, "Back off or I'll have your job. Don't ever touch me again."

Charlie dropped his hands to his sides but still his shape was stiff. He stood for some time watching John enter the councilor's center and the door shut behind him.

I watched Charlie go down to the edge of the water and untie a boat. He started to paddle away towards the far side of the Stepping Stone Islands.

I stepped closer to the edge of the water to see which way he went. The farther out he paddled the less I could make out of his direction. Then I gazed at the island that appeared larger than normal and thought for a moment I had seen a flash light shining around the water's edge. Perhaps it was nothing more than the moonlight.

I wandered back towards my cabin. My natural curiosity pulled my attention to thoughts of the island. The mystery was growing even stronger. What could John and Charlie be so angry about? Tomorrow was going to be another scavenger hunt for the younger kids. Somehow I was going to work that to my favor. I lay down curling up into my sleeping bag. Outside the window I could hear the branch scrapping across the glass.

The breeze had increased by morning but still the sun blistered through the window above my head. The cabin was empty and peaceful. Some distance away I could hear some kids yelling. I pulled my pants on and stepped outside. In the distance I could see Nyla and Lacey walking towards me.

"Hi Sam." Nyla looked towards the ground and shuffled her feet back and forth. Lacey stood twisting her pig tail into a tight knot. Nyla refocused her gaze towards my face as she played with her earrings before she said, "Have you been talking to Mack yet this morning?"

"No, I just got up. Where's he at?"

Nyla pointed a painted finger nail towards a small group sitting on the wharf. She looked towards Lacey who had wandered on towards the cabins. "I think you two best get it together before the scavenger hunt later today."

I stopped in at the lodge and grabbed a couple pieces of cold toast and gulped down some warm orange juice. Stepping back out on the front deck I noticed Mack and the group of kids were gone. I walked towards the basketball net because I knew it was Dakota's favorite place to hang out. Mack stood back from the small group with his hands pushed down deep into his pockets.

I walked towards Mack and stood next to him before I asked, "How was the bonfire last night, anything interesting happen? I'm sorry about not being there. I would have been bad company anyway."

"You don't have to be sorry for anything."

"I know. You don't either." I paused as I watched Carter take the ball from Dakota and pass it to Jacob in one real sweet move. They were pretty good and I knew if we wanted to win the competition next week I would have to make some time to practice.

"Let's go practice with the canoe. I've got something I would like to tell you about."

Once we put our vests on, we climbed into the canoe and moved off. There was something about being on the water and the sun above us that made things feel right. I think this was what I enjoyed most about camp so far. Mack started paddling hard and fast to get us moving.

I steered us towards the left side of the island. The two smaller Stepping Stone Islands came into sight before too long. The first stepping stone was about fifty feet long and had a rocky shore that reached towards the other island. The water between the two was very shallow.

I rested my paddle across the rim of the boat. "Mack, I do want to say that I would have loved to have knocked Hunter's block off last evening. It's just I don't want to be sent home for fighting. We can get back at him in other ways. I think we have a real good chance in beating the pants off them in the canoe challenge. Besides he's right I should try to set a good example for Dakota and the other younger kids.

"I understood more now because after you went to the cabin last evening Dakota, Carter and Jacob stuck to me. They had me drove crazy before the night was done. I understand how they look up to you now. You were right even if I would have loved to seen Hunter eat his words."

I smiled to myself and started to paddle again. Mack pushed on. It didn't take long and we were close to the Stepping Stone Islands. Twisting my paddle turned the front towards the rocky edge.

When the boat touched the bottom Mack turned towards me. "What's going on?"

I proceeded to tell him what I had overheard and saw the night before. Mack looked puzzled and said, "That's strange."

"I want to know more about this island. What's going on here anyway? My sister, Hanna Rae says I have a natural sense when it comes to a mystery. I've always loved a puzzle and this is a good one."

"But we're not allowed on Willie's Island." Mack's eyes appeared to have grown in size. He starred at the trees that loomed near the edge of the water.

"But...this isn't Willie's Island."

I pressed my lips together and stepped out of the boat into the shallow water by the edge of the canoe. We pulled the boat up onto the shore line and hide it under some bushes that were near the edge of the water. I tied it to one of the branches and looked towards Mack. He had pulled his safety vest off and flung it into the canoe.

The first twenty feet of the island appeared to be mostly swampy. Not far from there it became dryer and that's when the bugs found us. I pulled a small tube from my pocket and handed it to Mack. "Don't use much. Put some behind your ears and a bit on your hat. I picked it up at the lodge this morning."

Mack did as he was told then said, "So, what are we looking for?"

"I don't know. Mack if you're as good at puzzles as you think, then we'll know when we see it."

8

THE HULK

AFTER WE GOT BEYOND the swampy area the trees became thicker but very short. We trudged along until we came to a rocky path, which lead us more inland. I looked towards Mack as I wiped the sweat from above my eyes.

"Should we go farther? Looks like a road just beyond the next ridge of bushes." Mack pointed his plump finger.

Then within a moment we could hear something. It was a large heavy truck laboring along as if carrying a heavy load. I lowered my body down to the level of the bushes. Staying down we watched the truck move past us. The tarp that covered the back of the truck flapped in the light breeze.

"Well isn't that odd?"

Mack whispered, "Why would a big truck like that be out here in the middle of nowhere?"

"I don't know. The truck had no markings and I didn't recognize the men driving or I mean they're not from the camp anyway." I pulled out of my pocket a small red notebook. I scribbled some notes down even though the truck had no plates.

"I never heard tell of anything that was supposed to be going on over here." Mack looked straight at me. "Perhaps that's why this place is out of bounds."

I closed my notebook and slid it back into my pocket. "No one said anything about the small islands being out of bounds." I could hear another truck moving towards us and figured it would only be a matter of time and we would be spotted. "We better go. Perhaps we could come back after dark sometime."

Mack turned and slipped behind a nearby bush moving out of sight when suddenly I heard a deep voice boom over the sound the truck.

"Hey, you kid. Stop right there."

I wanted to run but I didn't want to look guilty of something so I stood my ground. Hoping Mack would be smart and stay out of sight, I stopped right where I stood. Feeling like my hair was standing up straight as a larger than large man approached me.

The man was covered with droplets of sweat. His well oiled muscles looked as big around as my head. His skin was well tanned and for some reason he had hair growing everywhere. The brown stained muscle shirt wasn't doing his muscles justice. His wide flat face appeared uneven with beady little eyes and no neck.

"What are you doing here kid?"

He had a two way radio hanging limply from a loop on his pants. It sounded like static as a raspy voice asked, "What's going on? You should be here by now."

His muscles appeared to budge as he smiled a toothless smile my way. He ripped the radio from his belt, up to his mouth. "I found myself a kid in the woods. Let the boss know."

Dropping the radio back to its spot his face glazed over with uncertainty. "What have you seen, anyway?"

I looked at my hands now starting to sweat. "I didn't see anything. What's with the big truck out here in the middle of nowhere?"

"Shut up kid. I'll ask the questions." He paused as if to collect his thoughts. A wide wrinkle lined the massive forehead then his eyes once more focused on me. "How come you're so far from your little camp?"

"I got mixed up in my directions. Looks like I turned the wrong way." I pulled my hand from my pocket and wiped the stress away from my own forehead. "I have to go now, Sadie the main counselor will be looking for me back in about ten minutes." I looked at my watch and realized it hadn't worked for the last few days.

The large man bent over leaning towards the bushes behind me. "Well I'm telling you if you know what's good for you, stay off the islands. I don't ever want to see your sorry face in front of me again."

With those words burned into my memory I turned and dashed out of sight. I was about fifteen feet away from him when I heard the static of his radio mixed with the message.

"The boss says to hold onto the kid."

The words gave me some power to move faster. I sprinted since I wanted to put some distance between me and the unknown. The small shrubs were easy enough for me to maneuver around. The large man had joined the chase. He sounded like the hulk plowing through the woods.

"Hey kid. Get back here the boss wants to speak to you. Stop right there!"

I didn't answer but continued to pick up speed. The sound of the hulk grew farther away as I pressed on. I could see Mack ahead of me. When I reached the canoe Mack had it untied. We pushed it out far enough that we were likely out of reach.

Mack looked startled as he watched the spot where we had cleared the bushy area. "What the hell was that all about?"

"He didn't sound like anyone that I wanted to go anywhere with. After I started to leave, the two-way radio told him to bring me in. Something about his boss wanted to see me. I imagine he'll be in big trouble."

"That's just what I thought. We'll be in big trouble when we get back to camp."

I looked at Mack and nodded. We turned the canoe heading back the way we came moving away from the island. After some distance I laid the paddle across the canoe and stopped to talk.

I paused before saying, "No one mentioned anything about someone working over there. It seems fishy to me."

Mack paused then said, "Well I guess to be honest, no one really has to explain things to us, do they."

"No, I guess you're right. The only thing is even that guy appeared to be very concerned about this island. He wanted to know what I had seen. That tells me there is something going on here that they don't want people to see."

We continued to paddle and soon arrived back to the dock. We tied the boat up and removed our vests leaving them in the boat. Then we noticed Sadie walking towards the edge of the dock.

"Where were you boys at?" She lifted her hand over her eyes to stop the glare of the sun. Then she shifted to look towards the island.

I spoke up before she could say anything else. "We were out practicing for the canoe challenge."

She smiled before saying, "I think we have some good teams this year."

Mack spoke up before I could say anything. "Sadie, why is Willie's Island out of bounds?"

"Out of bounds, it's not."

"We were told it was out of bounds."

"Well some of the counselors tell the younger kids that because we don't want people wandering over there without an adult." Sadie turned to walk towards the lodge. "As a matter of fact we're planning an overnight camping trip to the big island on Thursday night."

Once she was some distance from us Mack swiveled back towards me. "Sadie isn't too concerned about the island."

I felt the hair on the back of my neck prickle up. "First of all, Sadie doesn't know the things we've seen. The big hulk that just chased me isn't normal. Besides, no one called her to complain about us being on the island." I stepped around Mack and headed towards our cabin. "There's something going on there and you can't tell me you don't feel the same way. After all if they are up to no good they wouldn't want to contact the camp."

"Hey Mack… Sam."

We both turned to see Nyla running towards us. Her hair was all trimmed off and dyed black making her green eyes stand out even more. We both stood watching her as she tipped her hip from one side to the other. "Well, tell me do you like it? It's my real color. One of the counselors, Jane, helped me. She's doing Lacey right now."

I sputtered out, "What happened, I mean how come?"

With the long purple hair gone Nyla ran her hand up over her head. "It feels great and I know Mom will love it." She gazed towards us. "Come on you guys get with the program," she bugged her eyes out then pressed her mouth into a disappointed look as she said, "tomorrow…"

I said nothing and Mack grunted. I didn't have any idea what she was talking about.

"Tomorrow is family day and I'm looking forward to seeing Mom. What about you guys?" She reached up to give her earrings a slight tug. "Have you heard from your families? Is anyone coming?"

Mack dropped his chin and started talking to the ground. "Well I'm not sure but somehow I don't think Mom will let an opportunity slide where she can put her precious twins in the spotlight. They'll probably all be here."

Nyla frowned and then shone her eyes my way. "Well?"

"I'm not sure if Dad will be here, but I know Mom will be here for sure. I thought it was next week, week three."

"Honestly, you guys have been so absorbed in this island mystery. This is week three. You both look sweaty, where were you two anyway?"

I told Nyla about the smaller island and the unmarked trucks that we had seen. She was surprised to hear about the hulk. Then I told her about the sleep over.

Looking toward Mack, I said, "I think maybe that night we should sneak away to find out just what's going on there." Mack starred at me but said nothing.

I looked towards Nyla's sparkling green eyes and asked, "Well what do you think? Why wouldn't they tell us about the island activities instead of saying it's out of bounds. Furthermore what about John ordering us back to camp that day, like we had ticked him off, big time?" I ran my hands up through my hair as I looked at how short Nyla's hair was now.

Nyla stood still then shook her head. "I don't think I'm going wandering around the woods after dark. I mean I don't like heights or the dark woods. Don't look so disappointed I can be your look out at the camp site."

Mack had pulled his T-shirt off and appeared to be thinking about something else. "I'm going to change. The swimming hole is calling my name. The water must be warm enough by now."

Nyla rubbed the back of her neck before touching base with her earrings then said, "Mack it's almost lunch time. How long have you two been gone?"

Mack winked at Nyla and said, "If there's one thing I like better than swimming it's eating." He patted his stomach and laughed.

They both turned and headed towards the lodge as I continued for the cabin. Tomorrow was family day. I was looking forward to seeing Mom but the summer camp thing had really turned out to be a blessing. Time was flying by and I had made some good friends. The activities were great. I hadn't spent a lot of time thinking about Connor like I had when I was at home.

I put my swimming trunks on and headed back out the door. Then I noticed Charlie Chip heading out the road in a truck. The dust billowed up behind the truck as he gunned it hard. He was a strange man. It wasn't hard to tell he didn't care for kids of any age.

I walked into the lodge and found Nyla sitting with Mack. He was shoveling the food down with both hands. I turned my head when he smiled because I could see what was for lunch.

"I just saw Charlie Chip going like a dog on fire out the yard." I flopped down on the bench beside Mack. Reaching past Nyla I grabbed a roll and stuffed it into my mouth.

Mack stopped chewing and looked towards me then shook his head. He swallowed hard and gulped down a mouth full of apple juice. "Charlie Chip, so what?"

"I don't know but for a cook he seems very active around camp. I mean doing things not related to cooks and such. Maybe someone reported to him about catching me on the smaller island."

Mack stood up and looked directly at me. "I'm going to get my trunks on and I'll see you at the swimming hole… I mean if the mystery can wait for a bit."

Nyla lurched up from the table swinging her hand and laughing out loud before saying, "There's Lacey. I'll see you guys later on."

When I left the lodge I found myself feeling like I was the only person that was even concerned about the island. What was really going on there? I sauntered over towards the rope swing, under the maple tree that spread its branches to one side of the swimming hole.

I sat watching the others yelling and jumping in and out of the water. Dakota had become an awesome swimmer in the short time at camp. The mystery was an added bonus to help pass the time. Of course it could turn out to be a nightmare.

I had several letters from Mom but was really looking forward to seeing her the next day. I would have to be sure not to mention the mystery on the island to anyone tomorrow. Perhaps I could find out more info from Dad after all he knew about the camp from years ago.

Nyla and Lacey arrived with their towels for the swimming afternoon. Nyla's new hair due did help her blend into the group better. Still, her confidence and mannerisms had a way about making her stand out.

The family day had most of the campers on edge but the counselors had made plans that couldn't fail. Somehow I felt guilty that the mystery was the main reason for wanting to speak to dad.

While I was thinking about the next day I took notice of a canoe coming into sight from the far side of the little islands. You could imagine my surprise as the boat came closer to the dock. I noticed that it was Charlie Chip. It hadn't been more than two hours since I seen him burning his way out of the camp yard in a truck.

9

FAMILY ONCE MORE

LATER THAT EVENING I took notice of the wind howling around the trees outside and whistling through the knotholes in the walls. The watch that was strapped around my wrist shone brightly but wouldn't tell me the proper time. I found myself waking up several times glancing at the window for the first signs of early morning. My mind kept reworking the island and all its mysteries. Perhaps before the day would be done I would have more pieces to the puzzle.

I was anxious to discover the mystery of the island but my mind kept shifting back to the family day not far away now. I still felt inside like a little kid wanting and waiting to see my mother. I felt uneasy as if I could have forgotten the shape of her face, the look and feel of her hands. I was so disconnected from her and all that I had ever known.

I could hear someone shutting a door not too far from our cabin. The wind carried the sounds my way. I could tell from the tone of the voices they were angry. Mack was breathing heavy so I reached over and gave him a good shove. He rolled over and resumed his breathing but not as loud.

I raised myself up from my bed and tried to peer through the darkness. It only took moments as my eyes adjusted to the light and dark shades cast by the moonlight. It was John and even from this distance I could make out Sadie's shape. She shook her finger at him and he retaliated with his chest puffing up above her shoulders. She spun around on her heals and headed back to the councilors quarters. John walked towards the wharf disappearing into the night somewhere close to where the canoes were tied. His shape blended into the darkness as it spread thicker in the distance. The night air was mixed with the noise of the frogs and crickets.

I lowered myself back into bed. My mind shifted back to thinking about camp and my father. The anger that I had felt, before I went to camp, had fallen away. It had all been such a blessing. The mystery consumed my attention most of the time. It sure beat hanging around home bored with Connor being gone forever.

I can't say how long it was before I drifted back to sleep. The next time I opened my eyes I stared intently at two dirty feet, short stubby toes and all, not far from my face. It took several moments before I realized it was Dakota standing on the edge of my bed peering out the window.

"What time is it?" My voice was hoarse as I rubbed my sleepy eyes.

"If my watch is working it's about 6:32." Dakota talked loud enough to wake the rest of the cabin up. "I can hardly wait to see my Uncle Tom."

"Isn't your Mom coming today?"

"Yea, but Uncle Tom is more fun. In my last letter from Ma, she said he will be driving her here."

"I think my father is coming with my Mom too. Her last letter didn't say for sure. It did say they had something to discuss with me, something important." I rubbed my eyes once. "I'm still tired. I should try to get some more sleep." Doubling my pillow under my head I closed my eyes once more. My mind threatened to wake up completely as I said, "I heard John and Sadie arguing late last night so I didn't sleep real well."

"What were they arguing about?"

"I couldn't tell but I know from the look of the finger shaking that Sadie was put out at him."

Dakota jumped down from the edge of my bed. "I don't like him either. I've noticed she's often looking for him." He twisted around and looked at the others sleeping. "As a matter of fact I heard her say this was going to be his first and last year."

I had the feeling John didn't really like camp much. He never seemed to be around when he was needed. Then as my mind started to reboot I asked, "Does your Uncle Tom know much about the island?"

"The big island, Willie's Island, yea, he used to fish around here before the camp was even built." Dakota pulled his pants on and twisted his t-shirt over his head.

"Would you ask him, what happened to the people that lived in the house on the island, Willie's Island?" Then as an after-thought I decided to mention, "Don't let on I asked. I don't want any of the grown-ups to think there is anything going on."

"I didn't know there was a house." Then Dakota clamped onto the front of his pants and proceeded to do a bit of a dance before my eyes. "Can I go to the big lodge now, Captain Sam?"

I nodded my head and rolled back over thinking perhaps I would be able to catch at least another half hour. The door creaked as he opened then shut it hard.

I hugged my pillow and looked at the wall. I wondered what mom wanted to discuss with me. Without any more thought I could feel my muscles start to relax as I drifted back to sleep.

I woke to a loud clanging sound from the main lodge. Mack raised his head then flopped back down with a grunt. That's right; Nyla had told us the counselors were going to wake everyone for breakfast early today. She said they wanted everyone spit and polished before the parents started to arrive.

Reaching over I pulled my cleanest pair of shorts from under my bed. They felt stiff, but would have to do. I scratched my head and tried hard to flatten my hair down. When I stood and looked in the small triangle of mirror propped up by the lockers I realized there was nothing, nothing I could do about my hair. Mack grunted and pulled his same pants on from the day before. He sat on the edge of his bed dusting his hat off. Pulling his sleeping bag back up from the floor, he sighed then stood up looking at the door.

"I'm really not looking forward to this day of twin terror."

"Well I would, if I were you, try to let on like it doesn't matter." I gazed toward Mack's puffy face and asked, "Does it really matter?"

"Neither you or Nyla understand. She's an only child and you're the baby of the family." Mack stood now and rubbed his shoulder. "I think my parents are scared to spend some time with just me, only me. They likely think I'm really boring. Perhaps if I'm really lucky they will decide not to come, stay home and spend some extra time with the twins."

After most of the campers were done eating Sadie briefed everyone on the activities for the day. The day was shaping up to be pretty good especially the ball game with the parents. First of all when they arrived the campers were allowed to show the parents around the camp.

When I first noticed Mom and Dad approaching I was filled with mixed emotions. Before they took notice of me they were holding hands. Then as Mom saw me she picked up the pace and dropped his hand. Rushing towards me she wrapped her arms around me and hugged hard. Still trapped in Mom's embrace Dad stepped up and grabbed my hand giving it a good firm shake. I could feel an involuntary action as my lips spread into a genuine smile.

"We've missed you Sam." She twisted around as she gazed at all the buildings and the crowds of people. "Wow what a camp!"

I looked at Mom like I was seeing a new person. Her hair was newly curled and her face looked well rested. Her normal creases from worry had softened. Dad's head was on a swivel and he was smiling a lot. They were both very pleased to see me. I didn't have any anger, it was strange but the resentment of being sent away had left me.

"The old camp looks a lot different than when I was here. Of course we're talking about quite a few years ago." Dad looked down at the ground and bumped his shoes together. "How's the food Sam? Are they treating you good?"

I looked directly into his eyes and for the first time I allowed myself to see the concern that he tried to hide. Mom stood looking at the side of my head and then she reached up and pushed my hair down.

"Looks like the hair grew in pretty good over your stitches. I brought some new clothes for you. A couple pairs of shorts and a few clean T-shirts. Don't let me forget to take your laundry back with me."

I looked at them both and decided to come clean. "Camp has been great. I'm getting along good. I've made some real good friends. They call me Captain Sam." I lowered my head and then pulled my chin up straight as I locked eyes with Dad. "I didn't like being sent away. I was severely pissed off for some time. I guess it was still better than staying at home after Connor moved away and all."

Dad paused then pulled his shoulders back as he said, "We love you Sam. I can honestly say we've both missed you very much." He looked towards the lodge then back again, "Your mother let me read your letters. I'm really glad things have worked out for you. I didn't really like going against what you wanted. I figured it would be good once you got here in the woods and the fresh air."

I took them for the grand tour. Mom felt like the sleeping quarters were too bare, and concerned about the weight that I appeared to have lost, at least in her eyes. All in all, the morning was moving right along.

I noticed Mack coming toward me with his parents. His father walked with his hands in his pockets and his mother held unto her sun hat that flapped in the light breeze. I looked but couldn't see any twins in sight.

"Hey Mack," I waved my arm and beaconed them to come towards us. They came closer and I introduced them to my parents. "Where are the twins?"

Mack smiled and then said, "Mom and Dad came alone."

His mother stepped forward and still holding unto the top of her hat said, "This camp is all about Mack, the twins are at home."

Mack turned a bit red around the neck and couldn't help but smile. The parents struck up their own conversation. Things were going good and I even noticed them all laugh several times.

At one point I noticed Nyla rush towards a woman that had just arrived. There was no question it was her mother. She had the same swagger as Nyla and came across as needing to stand out in her own way. Her mother beamed as she stood beside her daughter. It was almost lunch time before I got a chance to introduce Mom and Dad to Nyla and her mother.

I explained to them how we were a great team and hoped to win the canoe challenge before the end of camp. Dad was very interested in the challenge. I proceeded to tell him about it while Mom had gone into the lodge with Nyla's mother.

"Mack has a good strong arm and with Nyla being small enough means we're not carrying a lot of extra weight. She's real fast on her feet and I must say a quick thinker."

Dad raised his hand to shade his eyes as he looked towards the big island. "It's some time before the ball game. Sadie said we could take a canoe for a paddle, how about it?"

I turned and looked directly at Dad now but he was still gazing off in the distance. A few butterflies took flight from my stomach navigating a way into my chest. The day was warming up to be a first in so many ways. "Yea, ok, I would like that."

We both put on our life jackets and I picked out my favorite canoe. I waved to Mom who was now sitting on the edge of the front deck of the lodge with Nyla's mother. She waved back and didn't even offer to move. I was looking forward to showing dad how good I was at maneuvering the canoe.

We weren't too far from the shoreline when he turned to look at me. "Boy, you're pretty good, been doing lots of practicing, eh."

I tried to hide my smile but failed miserably. I paddled hard for some time not wanting to say anything. I steered the canoe towards the far right of Willie's Island. I said, "This is the route for our final canoe challenge."

Dad sat with his back to me. I took notice of the way his shirt pulled tight across his shoulders. It wasn't long before I could see the material glisten as he worked hard. We crossed the lake fast with a real easy motion. Every here and there he would stop and look to one side or the other. That's right too, he would know about the islands from years ago.

"How many years ago did you come here?"

Dad stopped paddling and gazed up at the sun above, then shook his head. "I'm not sure how many years it's been. I came the first year it opened. A few years later, I was a student counselor. Do they have any mentor counselors now?"

"No. I think they were replaced with the captain idea." Then I paused for I knew I wasn't as good as having more experienced counselors. "I guess I'm learning as I go. It's been great though"

I paused laying my paddle across the edge of the boat. The water pressed around the bow as we glided slowly to a stop. The stillness in the middle of the lake was all consuming. Neither of us motioned to start moving again. I looked around, listening to the hustle at the camp. Then I noticed dad was just as mesmerized.

"I never realized how much I've missed this whole feeling of camp." He turned and glanced my way before he continued. "Funny the things I've noticed even the smell of the air and the feel of the breeze on my skin. I love the sounds of camp and the laughter."

"It's been great, I have to say. I've never even camped out before. There's always something new to discover. One day we were looking for a new route to get around Willie's Island, you know for the challenge, and we found an old sandbar on the back side of the island not far from the old house. Mack and I were thinking it would give us an edge over the other teams in the final challenge." I looked at dads back before continuing. "The old house is deserted now. Actually it's falling down. Did you know the people that lived there?"

"Yea, old man Harry Wiser and his wife, Anne lived there for years. She grew up and lived there most of her life. They had one son, Willie. The island used to be called Fisher Island then was renamed after their son."

"Where did the son go?"

"It was a big shock cause he drown in the lake, wasn't even ten years old. That was some time ago, a few years before the camp was even started. After the camp started up, well some kids seem to think the big island was haunted."

I twisted my paddle and aimed the front of the boat towards the far edge of the land that jutted out to a point. "What happened to the old people? I mean the house is nothing but ruins now."

"My uncle used to take me fishing there when I was younger, big lake trout, biggest I ever seen, over there by the dark side of that land jutting out. After the drowning most people stopped even fishing the waters."

He pointed a long finger towards a few darkened spruce trees that hung close to the waters' edge. Then he stared intently at the island before he continued. "Around the time their son died there was a man in town that tried to buy them out. Word was the other man almost hounded Harry Wiser to death."

I stopped steering again and rested my arms. I wanted to hear more but didn't want to come across as needing to know for any particular reason. I heard a loud cheer drift over the water to where we were resting.

Dad looked back at the camp and then motioned towards the sun. "Best be getting back, I think they have a family ball game planned."

"What happened to the old people?" I dipped my paddle into the water and pushed us around with a few twists and dad added his paddle to the motion. "What did the other man want the land for?"

"I don't really know. His wife took a bad fall after that and spent some time in the hospital. Old man Harry traveled back and forth for awhile. He often spoke about going south. For her health he always said."

Dad started to pick up speed with his paddle as the air turned silent for a bit. I thought he was done then out of the blue he said, "His wife always said she would never leave the island because her son's spirit was still there. Then one day word came they both disappeared. No one saw them again. I figured they went south."

"Did that other man buy the land in the end?"

"Well I guess. He moved into town and bought up the whole area. His name was Jack Stead. He's a lawyer and likely the only one with enough money."

"I think his son goes to camp here. His name is Hunter Stead." We approached the shoreline closest to the wharf and I managed to tuck the canoe back into the spot where it came from. My mind was filled with twice as many questions as I had before.

10

HOME RUNS

ONE OF THE MAIN events for the day was a ball game. We were all eager to start the game. There was a good mix of campers plus some of the parents. My dad and Mack's father were the only men on our team. I took notice that Hunter's father took off his suit jacket to play on Hunter's team.

Since there were four teams we had a sort of play off. In the end it was Hunter's Lone Wolf team against my team the Angry Coyotes. Hunter had his team mates whipped into a frenzy, even though he couldn't hit the ball himself. Most of the parents were trying their best but for some reason they acted like it was only a game. One thing I had learned from camp was that everything meant something.

When the last game of the playoffs was ready to start, Hunter won the toss catching the tip of the bat with the ends of his long slender fingers. Hunter raised his eyes up to meet mine and curled his lip up before saying, "I'm always first, remember that."

I looked straight into his face as I said, "I gave it to ya! Besides, to be the last team up gives me an edge."

Hunter's team was good there was no doubt about it. The feeling was it would go right down to the wire. Hink and Dink were the strongest players on his team. Hunter couldn't hit his way out of a wet paper bag but he knew that and played with his strengths. I had to give him credit; he was the brains behind the game.

The game moved along fast and the score was tight. They started out with three runs but we caught up and passed them at the end of the first inning with a score of four, three in Coyotes favor. The start of their second inning the score floated at a tie for a bit. They dug in hard and pulled ahead by two more runs making the tie only a memory.

I must say Hunter did well and at the last minute pulling ahead to six, four. The game was in Hunters favor now. The end of the second inning we squeaked by with only two more runs. Hunter had a pleased look to him as the teams switched places at the end of the second inning with a six, six tie. This was Hunters last chance and they drove us hard really working our outfielders. The top of the third inning we were sweating and still they pulled in a huge total of three more runs. The score was nine, six in his favor. I looked at my team hoping above all odds we had what it would take.

Most of the parents stood back holding up the part of being cheerleaders. Mack's father had struck up a good conversation with my Dad. I watched as Nyla gazed at my mother talking to hers. Nyla and Mack were the best on my team.

I understood it's not all about the best and I was sorry to see Carter and Dakota strike out. They looked heartbroken as I patted them on the back. I sent Mack up next and he squared off with Hunter pitching. Mack tapped the side of his sneaker with the bat and humped into a slouched position prepared for the worst.

Hunter wiped his forehead off with his sleeve. He gazed around his team and pointed Hink to the other side. Then his own father who was on third base yelled towards his son. "Let her fly man. This is going to be easy and fast."

Hunter refocused on Mack and smirked before letting the ball fly towards him at a break neck speed. It was one of the things that Hunter was indeed good at. The ball flew by Mack as he swung the bat too high.

"Strike One."

Sadie was the umpire and usually called it pretty even. She stood slouched behind the catcher. The large square block of a catcher was Dink. He slapped his hand into the catcher's mitt several times before yelling towards Hunter. "Good one. Come on, lay me another one right here, come to papa."

Mack walked away from the base for only a moment.

Mack's father yelled, "Come on son. Show him what you're made of."

Mack looked towards his father. He had often spoken of how he missed his Grandfather and the closeness they had always shared. Somehow he had been surprised to have them here at camp for him and only him.

Mack stepped up to the plate once more with a stronger sense of determination. Swinging the bat at the invisible target he clenched his teeth and focused his stare at the ball that would soon come into his vision. 'Keep your eye on the ball.'

Hunter delayed the windup and looked back over his team giving them all the evil eye warning them not to let him down. His eyes gazed over the outfielders then he stopped as he noticed his father watching him. Gradually he refocused once more on Mack's heavy-set form before him.

As the ball left his fingers Hunter's frame dropped with a released position that swept over him.

I starred at the ball coming fast towards Mack with a different type of spin on it. With a powerful stride Mack stepped forward one step and swung with all his might.

Crack… the sound echoed back towards the stand of trees in the distance. The first hit of last inning was a good one.

Mack slung his bat behind him, forcing Sadie to jump out of the way, as he sped towards the first base.

Hunter stepped towards the ball that drilled past him. Mack picked up speed before glancing to the outfielders. He pulled back and stayed at first base.

Nyla was next in line and spit on her hands in a fashion that I would expect from only her. Her short form pulled a tight swing moving nothing more than air. I knew if she had of connected, it would have been a good one.

"Take it easy sweetie." Hunter smirked as he continued to irritate my team with his smart remarks. "I'll give you a slow one. Take your time, here it comes."

Even from where I stood I could tell Nyla didn't like to be patronized.

Before the ball even went over the plate she lurched forward and sent it over towards the swimming hole. Hunter's father soon picked it up giving my team only a one base move. With first and second base loaded it was up to me to fill the bases or else bring them home.

I grabbed the bat and swung four or five mighty swings trying hard to loosen up my shoulders. I nodded my head towards Mack and stepped up to the plate. The smoothness of the wooden bat was cool in my hands. A light breeze lifted the hair off my damp forehead. I watched as Hunter moved back and forth starring my way, then turning to look at his teammates.

I stood and moved away from the plate for only a moment then stepped back into position and swung my bat a few more trips. The tension in my shoulders was almost overpowering my thoughts of trying to relax and watch the ball.

The ball was speeding towards me and the instant I swung the bat I knew it was too far out of range.

"Strike one." Sadie yelled to everyone.

I recollected myself and took a few deep breaths trying hard to refocus but relax at the same time. Seconds slide by fast before the ball twisted into my sight. I held my breath till I swung hard feeling like my arms were going to be wrapped around my rib cage forever but I only nicked the ball.

"Foul ball," Sadie said, "Take it easy Sam." She paused before yelling, "Play ball."

Hunter pushed his hand into his mitt and ever so slowly pulled his leg up into the air and spun the ball towards me. I watched as it slowed down in mid air then curved into the top of my arm. Smack. I dropped the bat and clutched my arm in pain.

The cheerleaders in unison voiced their disapproval, "Ohhh."

I hung onto my arm as I took notice of the smirk on Hunters face. Even from this distance I could tell he loved it. Dropping back away from the plate, I could feel the bruise welt up on the top of my arm. Hunter shrugged and yelled from where he stood, I'm sure for the benefit of the others. "Sorry man."

Sadie stepped forward to check out my arm. With a wave of her hand I was sent walking. The bases were now loaded.

I pointed at my father. He smiled as he twisted his hands together. Grabbing the bat he stepped up to the plate. He pulled his shoulders back and swung the bat hard for several practice swings. He stood for a moment and gazed towards the cheerleaders and nodded his head towards Mom. Hunter laughed and nodded at his own team members. He pointed to his father and moved him toward shortstop. Then he turned back and shook his head with a funny looking smirk.

Dink stood to stretch then buckled his knees as he prepared for the ball to blaze towards him. "Come on man. Put the ball right here." Hunter smiled as Dink smacked his hand into the glove over and over.

I stood watching as my father prepared to settle into the game. The wind puffed his hair up around his face. He looked in the distance as the sun sparkled off the water. He squinted as he dug his feet into the soft sand by home plate. Shifting his focus from the water on the lake towards Hunter he paused once or twice before stepping up to the plate for the final time.

Hunter rolled the ball over and over between his fingers. He was good at playing the game, not as good as my father but still good. He turned and once more looked over his team. Then his eyes settled on his father before shifting into the final movements. He pulled his leg up in the air for the windup. Leaving his fingertips the ball twisted, parting the air, shearing close to my father's head.

Dad pulled his shoulders in as he jumped back from the almost definite collision with the ball. He laughed making eye contact with Mom as he stepped forward for another chance to make it right.

Sadie stepped forward and yelled to Hunter, "Do you want someone to replace you?" Hunter shook his head and did his best to look sorry. Sadie looked down at Dink then yelled, "Watch what you're doing then. Ball one."

The next time the ball went sailing over the plate he swung a mighty swing and once more turned to smile towards mom.

"Strike one." Sadie bellowed adding to the tension of my team.

Dad took a few powerful practice swings then stepped in closer to the base. Hunter continued to check his team and delay the whole process allowing the tension to build. The next time the ball came swirling towards home plate Dad connected with the ball and for an instant I couldn't see where the ball went.

Before I was sure which way to look, Mack went speeding over home plate. Nyla ran a smooth trot around the bases and blew a kiss towards Hunter. I wallowed in the feeling of despair that hung around Hunter's neck as he refused to make eye contact with me. Dad's lean shape had no problems clearing the bases. The score was ten to nine in our favor. Everyone bounded up into the air as if their very life depended upon us winning the game. Perhaps it didn't matter to most of them who won just that the game was over.

Still I smiled at the simple fact that we had won the game and felt good about it. I hoped it was an omen that pointed towards the canoe challenge at the end of next week. The afternoon had stayed sunny and we all enjoyed ourselves. My best friends had met my parents and I had met theirs. Things had a way of working themselves out and the family day drew to a close.

There was a shadow of sadness to her mouth drooping around the edges for only a moment before Mom said, "I need to speak to you Sam."

"Oh yes, I almost forgot that you wanted to talk to me about something."

Dad stood up as he jingled his coins in his pocket before saying, "Jean, I'll give you two some time. Call me if you need me." With that he turned and walked away.

Mom said, "Let's sit over here at the picnic tables."

"What's going on Mom?"

Mom sat down and took to gazing at her folded hands now placed on her lap. She took a couple deep breaths and said, "Because I forced you to go to camp, I now want to give you the choice if you would like to come home with me today."

I stood up and looked around. Some of the parents had already left and the swimming hole was bubbling over with hot kids still reeling from the ball game. The sun was getting lower in the sky and the breeze was dropping down. In the distance the mystery of Willie's Island loomed ahead of me. Some of the canoes were now on the lake and other kids were starting to gather some wood for the bonfire that would happen at dark.

"No, I think I would like to stay. I don't want to let the other members of my team down; after all we still have some of the biggest challenges still to come."

Mom smiled and looked towards Dad in the distance. "I'm glad you've made some friends." Then she sighed again and patted the seat beside her. "I also want to tell you when you do come home from camp we'll already be moved to Onslow."

I stood once more and was lost for words. My mind swept back over the years I had spent above the second hand shop. To think I would never see home again created a chill deep into my soul. I somehow wanted to see things again, say goodbye to some of my other friends. I hung my head as I tried to grasp the shock of things.

Mom continued to talk as she lowered her voice. "I'm sorry Sam but I think it'll be easier this way."

Inside I felt like I was being pushed once more. I looked towards Mom and for the first time I realized it couldn't be much easier for her. Her face looked stiff and her eyes had a glassy look to them. Trying to push beyond my feelings towards understanding her thoughts was hard I must say.

Before I could even become accustomed to anything she blurted out, "Your father and I are getting back together. He'll be living with us when we move to Onslow."

I could feel my head spinning and a heat consuming my body as I turned to look towards Dad standing in the distance talking to Mack's father.

11

OUT OF CONTROL

"What, what are you saying?" I could feel my hands clench into tight fists. I twisted back around and looked directly into her eyes. I didn't waver from my stare. Mom stood unmoving, her emotions created a determination that saturated the air.

"That's why he wanted me off to camp, wasn't it?"

Mom continued to stare, her mouth didn't move. Her eyes darted back and forth over my face. "No, that had nothing to do with it."

"What I feel has no bearing on anything does it?" I looked down and kicked some dirt up into a pile. "So I guess it's all decided then." I puffed some hot air out of my lungs and returned my gaze deep into her eyes.

"Sam, stop it, be reasonable this will be better for all of us. For once in my life I will be able to give you something you've never had before, a complete family."

"I loved the family I had, the one that was always there when I needed them. Did you forget he left us, he didn't care what he left behind?"

"That was just as much my fault as his."

"I understand, but you stayed and he didn't. You did all the work and now I'm supposed to forgive and forget, act like nothing really happened."

"He's trying to make up for things. You forget, he does love you Sam. Besides, it's time for me to also think about myself for once. I'm tired of being alone."

The words appeared to give her some kind of strength as if hearing them out loud made it more real. She pulled her shoulders back and pressed on as she run her hands up over her face and rubbed her eyes.

"You can make up all the reasons you want, but it really has nothing to do with me. I understand that he's going to be living with us. I don't have to like it and I don't want anything to do with it. Don't bother to let on it's in some way for me."

"Stop it Sam. This is a new chapter to all our lives. It can be just as good as you want to make it."

Mom stopped and looked in the distance and then changed her tone. It had more of a pleading feel to it. "Please Sam, try to think of more than just yourself and help me rebuild the life that I should have had all along."

I stopped and looked at her face now creased with lines of concern around her eyes. There was a softness that formed around the edge of her lips. She closed her eyes and turned her back to me then just as quick she twisted back around with tears hanging onto the edges of her eyes. "This means a lot to me Sam. I've never asked for much for myself. I'm asking now to please, please just give this a chance for me, please."

The feeling inside started to slow down as I was drawn into her emotions that were now carved across her face. "I love you Mom. I'm sorry that I've made this so hard for you. All I can say is I don't like this but I'll try."

"Thank you Sam. JC and Hanna Rae will be home the weekend after we move to Onslow. Perhaps that will help you adjust a bit."

I looked down at the ground where I had been working hard at digging a hole with my sneaker. In the distance I saw Dad talking to Sadie. They appeared to be getting along pretty good. Finally he walked towards us. He didn't ask anything but Mom stepped forward with a half smile and looped her arm in his.

"Well it's time for us to go."

"Jean, please wait in the car. I'll only be a bit; I would like to talk to Sam."

Mom reached for me and hugged me hard. Then she pushed me back from her and looked into my eyes. A slight smile flickered up over her lips. She started to say something then hesitated, likely thinking better of it and turned to walk towards the car. We both watched as she climbed into the car in the distance.

Dad turned towards me and for once looked directly into my face before saying, "Sam I would like to say..."

"You had this planned all along, didn't you?"

"What, no I didn't.

"Well Mom might swallow that but I don't."

"Sam, listen to me." He pulled his hands from his pockets and looked towards the car where mom was now waving. "I've always loved your mother. I know now that it was wrong what I did... leaving all you behind. I did try to contact you, even wrote letters but your Mom stopped that. She had her own reasons which I couldn't really blame her."

"I understand that you will be living with us but I want you to know that I don't like it. How can we trust you? How do I know that you'll not just leave again someday for some unknown reason like before?"

"I don't blame you for your uncertainty Sam. All I want to say is that I'll continue to try and earn your respect." Dad now looked at the ground and the pile of dirt that I had been working at. "Try to enjoy the rest of camp. It's going to be all right Sam wait and see. We'll pick you up at the bus station in Truro when camp is done." Reaching his hand out towards me he held it in mid air for few more moments.

I looked at his hand then into his eyes but said nothing. He dropped his hand down and looked towards the car where Mom was waiting. "I enjoyed our time today. I mean in the canoe and the ball game. Thanks Sam for at least allowing me to be a part of that."

I watched as Dad walked away and wondered how I would ever get over my dislike of his actions. The car turned and I waved towards mom who was now hanging out the window. Slowly I walked towards the cabin and felt the weight of the day heavy on my shoulders.

In the distance I could hear the raised voices of the others as they prepared for the bonfire. When I reached the cabin Mack and Nyla were sitting on the steps smiling and laughing about the days events.

Nyla paused as I got closer, she stopped laughing before asking, "Why such a long face Sam?"

I told them about my big surprise. Inside I waited for their comments. I wondered how close we had really got. Could they understand how I really felt?

Mack looked down at the ground and kicked the bottom step with the toe of his sneaker. "It was nice knowing that my father wanted to spend more time with me, so I don't understand what the problem is."

"Well think about it. He doesn't want me it's mom he wants. I just happen to go along with things besides he could leave again anytime."

"That's right Sam. You are a package deal and he knows that. Perhaps that is part of what attracted him. Your Dad sounds like he's sorry for what happened and it's his only chance to make things up to you both." Mack looked up at Nyla waiting for her input.

Nyla pushed her hands up over her stubble of hair resting them on her earrings and smiled. "I would have given anything to have a father that wanted to get to know me better, make up for lost time." She looked at her hands now spread out before her eyes as she blinked away a glassy look. "I'll never have that because I don't even know who my father is. I think you should be glad for the second chance."

I looked at them both then stood up and pushed my hands into my pockets before saying, "I can see you guys just don't understand. I expected more compassion from my friends."

Nyla looked at Mack then back towards the bonfire. "I think you should think this through. This is a rare chance that so many kids will never have."

She looked at Mack once more and said, "Let's go, the bonfire it's about to start. You want to come, Sam?"

"No, I'm going to sit here for awhile and do some thinking. I wouldn't be good company anyway."

I sat outside and listened to the frogs sing and the kid's laughter breaking the silence every now and then. The night air was humid. In the distance I could hear thunder rumble over and over. I lost interest in even thinking so I went inside and climbed into my bed. Sometime later I heard everyone coming in to bed but kept my eyes closed. I heard Mack stub his toe on the edge of the bed. Dakota took a laughing jag as Mack danced around in circles.

The last thing I remembered hearing before I drifted off to sleep was Dakota asking Mack if there was really a ghost of a one armed man that lived on the far side of the sawdust pile. Was it also true the arm was in the pile of sawdust? Mack didn't help much by saying; no he thought that the ghost was on the big island.

Dakota sounded a bit shaken as he said, "Well tomorrow night we go to the big island camping." His breathing became a bit heavy before he finally asked Mack if he could keep his flashlight on for awhile.

The next morning I opened my eyes to see Carter and Jacob leaving for the main lodge. The door didn't latch after Dakota grabbed the handle ripping it open and swinging down off the step. The air was cooler this morning with a slight breeze drifting a smell of ashes towards me. The bonfire of the night before was well watered down leaving a sooty smell behind.

Rubbing my nose I focused on two people that stood behind the lodge. Even from this distance, I could tell from where I lay, it was John and Charlie Chip. They never appeared to get along. The thing was I could never figure out what they had in common to get riled up about. John being a counselor and not a very good one then there was Charlie being a cook that really didn't like kids. Then I noticed John shaking a finger at Charlie before he turned and strutted around the corner of the lodge and went straight down to the edge of the lake. Charlie stood still for some time then reached in his pocket and took out a set of keys. He walked straight to his truck and spun around in a quick circle leaving the yard.

I watched the dust billow up into the air. Grabbing my shorts out from under the bed I pulled them on quickly and headed out the door to see where John went. I rounded the corner of the lodge to find Mack and Nyla sitting on the edge of the step. In the distance I could tell John was headed in a canoe directly towards Willie's Island.

I walked towards Mack and Nyla and pointed towards John before asking, "Where's he going, do you know?"

Mack squinted towards the water and said, "I heard Sadie ask about the camping site on Willie's Island for tonight."

Nyla stood up and walked towards me. She touched my arm and made a funny face. "I'm sorry Sam for being so insensitive about your Dad and all."

"Yea, man, me too." Mack smiled then said, "It's hard to understand parents at the best of times. Let's forget about them and enjoy the rest of our time at camp."

I started to walk away and beckoned for them to follow. They both jumped up and moved along to catch up. We walked towards the wharf. I stopped to look around to see who was able to overhear us. "I want to find out, what's the big secret with that island. Later tonight, the first chance we get to slip away. I want to check around the old house for any clues as to what's going on."

Nyla stopped and looked directly at us. "What is it about that island? Both of you appear to be consumed with it." She looked down as she brushed some invisible dust from her shirt. "I'm not fond of going into the woods after dark." Then she paused as she watched John paddle out of sight. "Still, I don't want to be left behind. Count me in."

I held my mouth into a firm line. Studying both their faces I said nothing.

Nyla looked towards Mack and said, "Sam you weren't there last night when they told us the story about a ghost."

I laughed before saying, "The key word there is story."

Mack hesitated then with a slight twitch to his neck he nodded his head. "Don't matter much because I don't think we'll be able to get away tonight without being seen."

I thought for a minute, but knew we had to try. "We'll wait till everyone is asleep and then we'll sneak out. If anyone notices, we can say we went into the bushes to use the bathroom or something." I switched my gaze from Mack to Nyla trying to read her expression.

Her face was drained of color with a stiff serious look for a moment. "You'll have to toss a stone at the side of my tent or something when you're ready. We'll have to be careful."

It was a hot sweltering day and the swimming hole was the most popular place to be. There was a few smaller activities going on but for the most part we all were given a rest from the full day before.

It was about two o'clock in the afternoon and Sadie stopped us when we came out of the lodge. "Would you three help out and take some of these tents over to the big island for the camp-out? I can't seem to locate Charlie Chip today. I better call for a replacement."

"Yea sure. We could use the practice with the canoe anyway." I turned and smiled at Mack who was busy looking towards the island. Nyla reached over to grab one of the smaller bundles then gave Mack a kick to bring him back to life.

Taking hold of one of the heavy bundled up tents Mack headed towards the canoes behind Nyla. Mack stumbled because he was still starring at the island.

I tried to carry two bundles but dropped one after only a second. Catching up with Mack and Nyla, I asked, "Where could Charlie Chip have gone? What are you looking at anyway?"

"Do you see over by the far right side by that large droopy pine? See the big tree that hangs over the water's edge." Mack pointed towards the far side.

"Putting my bundle down and raising my hand over my eyes I looked in the direction that he said. What am I suppose to be looking for?"

"I thought I seen someone over there. It looked like Hunter."

"Likely he has taken some parcels over for Sadie."

"No because the overnight campout is over here more in the middle of the front edge of the island. There would be no need for him to go that way."

I collected up my parcels and started to move towards the wharf. The water was a mirror of the blue sky above. Nyla dropped her bundle and climbed into the middle of the boat. The noise of the lodge was left behind, nothing more than the dip of our paddles into the clear water.

Mack looked around the area then broke the silence as he said, "I love this camp. It's been great and I think we all should try to come back each year till maybe we can get a job as a counselor. I know we don't even have two weeks left and I really hate to see it end."

"Yea, I was thinking the same thing the other night. It wouldn't be the same without you or Nyla here. Let's speak to Sadie sometime to find out what kind of training we would have to have."

Mack smiled from ear to ear. "Great."

Nyla clapped her hands as she smiled.

Getting closer to the island we glided towards the landing site for the camp. About ten feet away the bushes rustled and out popped Hunter. He had an uncomfortable look to him, strange to see him without Hink and Dink. Upon seeing us he pulled his shoulders back and run his hand through his hair removing some twigs.

I noticed a canoe shoved into the edge of the bushes. I asked, "What are you doing over here?"

"None of your business… I was just checking out the camp area… besides all the land around here plus this island belongs to my father." Hunter looked down his long thin nose and gave us the feeling like it was below him to even speak to us. He tugged on his boat and was soon moving back towards the lodge.

12

A LONG NIGHT

MACK UNCLENCHED HIS FISTS. He puffed out his breath as if he had just run a big race. "I hate that guy."

Nyla laughed a light hearted sound as she tugged on her earrings and then said, "Mack you take him too serious. The way you act reinforces the fact he thinks he's important. Forget him."

"That doesn't sound like the right attitude for a camp counselor." I tried to hide the amusement that I felt with the look that spread over Mack's face now. "I know what you mean though."

We laughed as we climbed out of the canoe and tied it to a droopy bush. Pushing through the thickness of the bushes we tugged the bundles by the corners. Ten feet from the shoreline was a large clearing surrounded by tall dark towering spruce. Several flat areas were scuffed clear of any larger sticks. In the middle of the clearing was a circle of charred rocks for the evening campfire. The bed of ashes once stirred had a wet sooty smell that lingered in the still air. To one side was four or five large picnic tables propped up with some old bricks. The tables were weather beaten and standing at a tilt but for the most part would do. I turned and looked back towards the lodge. We stood on a higher piece of land and I could see above the bushes by the edge of the water. Hunter was nowhere in sight between here and the lodge. I scanned the surface of the water but still saw no canoe.

I compared notes with Mack and Nyla on things we had overheard Sadie and John discussing the evening before. It wasn't hard to tell that John didn't like the idea of an overnighter, on the big island, one little bit. Sadie was the main organizer of the overnight trip. Against John's wishes he was told to stay at the main lodge to help the younger campers with other plans. Mack heard him say that the big island was too dangerous. If anyone got hurt then it would be a hard job getting medical help. Sadie looked long and hard at John then walked away.

It wasn't long before the canoes arrived with the rest of the campers. The noise of the island wasn't noticed over the chatter of the group. The supplies were piled up beside the tables and fire wood was collected for the evening ahead. The tents were still piled in one spot and it was getting later. Before too long one final canoe pulled up to the edge of the island.

Sadie noticed the shape coming through the bushes close to the group. Then she said, "This is Brian Hart. He drove the bus bringing some of you to the camp. He's agreed to stay the night to help out with the cooking and other arrangements. Brian is from the area and spent many years of his youth here. He has a story to tell about the island and how it got its name."

Brian's thin hair had been removed from the usual ponytail and hung down limply around the edges of his face. His wide flat nose was very white almost in an unnatural way. Sunk deep into the thousand wrinkles of his face were the darkest black eyes I had ever seen. When he laughed it was a hard forced sound. Spaced between his thin lips were stained teeth. His shoulders were small and slouched forward. When he wasn't talking he motioned with a continuous rubbing action of his hands. His clothes looked raggedy and those were holes I saw in his sneakers.

Things settled into an evening full of excitement even though the wind pulled dark clouds over head. I must say though Brian did know loads about camping and moved with such speed helping to get all the tents up. The food tasted even better, being cooked outside. I think Brian was a better cook than Charlie Chip. You know it's hard to beat a hot dog on a stick.

The darkness was creeping in around the edges of the trees. The sound of the frogs made me feel like they were getting closer and closer. Brian stood up and picked a few pieces of wood and threw them on the fire. He stood for a few moments and appeared to be looking over the group. When his eyes lit on me he smiled a crooked wrinkled smile and nodded his head. Then he looked towards Sadie and asked in a low voice, "It's getting late, should I start the story now."

Brian paused appearing distracted as he looked towards the forest that loomed behind us. He took a large stick and stirred the fire for a bit. The sparks flared up into the night air.

"Ok now I'm going to tell you a story that has made many people leery of this island. Many people that used to hunt and fish this area stopped. They never come back here and as much as I've tried they won't come with me."

He looked at Sadie they pulled his hair back away from his face. The fire flared up and appeared to deepen the wrinkles that aged him. "I warned Sadie about doing this overnight camp thing." He walked over towards her and stood tall and thin above her. "This story I'm about to tell you, well she doesn't believe it."

Sadie stood beside Brian now with a wide smile, her teeth glistening in the light of the fire then said, "I've heard the story before and I know that my Grandmother swears by it. I sort of like to have proof, you know before I will fall pray to any fear."

"Ha, its proof you want is it. Well after this night you may wish you didn't ask for such proof. The spirits of this island are all around us." He humped his shoulders down and glanced sideways from one side to the other.

He stopped talking and quickly turned to look behind himself towards the edge of the forest. He slouched down and touched Dakota who was closest to him. Dakota snapped his flashlight on shocking himself. Brian's eyes looked like glass in the light of the fire. He whispered to Dakota in a shaky voice, "Whatever you do, don't go into the forest."

Sadie suddenly stood, stretching and said, "Well I'm off to bed. Everyone knows where to sleep. Goodnight."

I said, "Goodnight" the other voices chimed behind mine and then all eyes were refocused on Brian.

Brian waited till Sadie was in her tent and her flashlight out. His eyes shone as he stirred the fire once more. "You all have time to run to your beds now, if you like, if you're too scared."

I looked around and although some appeared uneasy no one stood or motioned to leave. Slowly Brian made eye contact with each one of the campers. When his face looked my way, he winked. I can't say for sure, perhaps he winked at each one of us. His voice got lower as his story started.

"You best all sit closer to the fire. Pull your knees up tight to your chest to be safe." He once more looked behind himself. A sloshing noise made him quickly snap around to look towards the water.

Gradually he seated himself down so close to the fire I thought his sneakers smelled hot and stinky. Mack was pushed as close to my elbow as possible. I swear Nyla was hugging Mack from what I could see.

"In the beginning this was called Fisher Island. It was one of the best places to fish for miles around. There was a family lived on this island, a husband and wife that loved each other as much as they loved their island. They stayed to themselves most of the time and only came to town for very few supplies. Years passed and finally word came that they had a son named Will.

I think the boy was about ten when I heard there was a group of big wigs that wanted the island and all the land around here. People say they put a lot of pressure on the family to sell. Everyone felt like Will was obsessed with the island and anything to do with it. I have friends, good friends that swear the boy was violent when he caught anyone hanging around or being nosey."

At this moment Brian stood up and gazed towards the trees for several moments before he resumed his story. Every time he turned to look into the darkness that surrounded us Dakota was being pulled into the story.

Brian lowered his voice once more before saying, "I think we'll be safe enough tonight, I mean as long as the moon stays out. The fire needs to be kept going, I mean all night."

It was as if he knew the moon was going to be hidden before long. In the distance I heard a gunshot and the noise vibrated down the row of campers.

Dakota stood up quickly and said, "What was that Brian?"

Brian pulled his hair back away from his face and starred into the darkened area away from the water's edge. He tipped his head sideways and listened. His voice wavered as he said, "I imagine it was a car back firing in the distance. As the crow flies we're not too far from the Trans Canada." He pointed a long skinny finger into the darkness on the other side of the island.

The campers settled down again, some focused on the fire and some squirmed as they kept glancing back behind them.

In the distance between here and there I heard an owl hoot. Returning my gaze towards Brian I settled back down for the rest of the story. I wanted to hear more about this boy that my dad had also mentioned to me. Brian and Dad had been old friends so I figured likely there was some truth to the story we were going to be told.

Brian rubbed his face as if to straighten out some of the wrinkles. He had no success in that so he seated himself at the end of the log facing most of the campers.

"Well the man and his wife lived pretty well but the boy took it upon himself to help protect them. I mean anytime he caught someone fishing around the island he would set traps. They say he left people hanging upside down for hours at a time."

Brian paused and I couldn't tell if it was special effects or perhaps he was trying to pick his words to continue the story. He stood up and stirred the fire once more. The sparks snapped and cracked and took flight. I gazed up into the darkness as the moon disappeared behind some clouds. Then as if on cue we all looked at each other. There was a noise like someone rushing through the bushes from the edge of the water towards us.

Brian grabbed a large stick and stepped towards the noise. Then Hunter came bursting through the bushes with Hink and Dink right behind him. They appeared to have a look of relief to see us all around the fire. Brian never cared for Hunter and his response at seeing them was as I would have expected.

"What the heck! Where did you guys come from?" Brian cleared his throat and tried to sound tougher.

Hunter now collected himself and said, "We told John we changed our minds. We wanted to be a part of the camping trip."

Brian looked annoyed but dropped his stick on the fire and said, "Well I was just telling them the story about the boy,

Will." He looked toward Hunter before saying, "You know the story well I expect."

Hunter looked down his long thin nose right at me. I could feel Mack stiffen up as his eyes met Hunters.

Hunter already had a bored look to his face as he said, "Oh great we just arrived at story time. What a thrill."

Brian stepped forward and said in a deep stiff voice as he looked directly into Hunter's face, "Well we're not very thrilled with having to put up with you either. All I can say is go back to the lodge if you don't like our company. I don't imagine anyone here will protest."

Hunter looked out over the water before sitting down with no other comments. I turned my attention back to Brian and hoped he would pick the story back up where he had left off. Most of the other campers also appeared to be interested in what happened to Will.

Brian said, "Oh yes, I was saying how Will had gotten pretty rough with some of the other locals. A couple of my buddies were hurt, broken arms and the need for stitches, things like that. He cut them down and told them in no un-certain terms to tell everyone to stay away from his island."

Brian rubbed his chin for a moment as he looked above at the sky. "This went on for some time till Will's mother had to be put into the hospital with some bad bruises. My mother worked at the hospital and said that the old woman looked like someone that had been mugged."

"Time passed and things kept getting worse and worse. One day the unthinkable happened, Will was found dead. Some say he was caught in one of his own traps, others say that he was beaten up by the men that wanted the land."

Brian turned with his fists clenched and looked towards Hunter.

Hunter pulled his shoulders back and said, "That old story, my dad says it was an accident how that boy died. They should have sold the land when they got the first offer. Perhaps they would all be alive even now."

Brian ran his tongue over his lips as he starred hard at Hunter before saying, "Yea, you would know wouldn't you." He turned his head and looked towards the trees behind me. His eyes shone black and I could swear I seen hate and revenge flicker up over the wrinkles on his face. "The man and woman never got over the death of their son. The locals renamed the island, Willie's Island, because most believed the son's spirit was still here protecting their island. Thing was, after some time the woman's health seemed bad and there was talk that perhaps they would move down south."

Jacob stood up before the fire. The side of his face was reddened from the heat of the fire. Carter followed his motions as he shivered before saying, "My mom says this place is haunted and the boy doesn't like people being on the island. She says his ghost still sets up traps and some people have been hurt here but can't explain what happened."

Brian put his hand on Carter's shoulder and pushed him back into his seat. "Then one day some time after the death of their son they moved away without any word to anyone. I think that was when the land was sold and the big wigs got their way in the end."

Hunter snickered as he looked toward Hink and Dink. "It was a good deal, my dad said. It doesn't look like much to me."

Brian's eyes had glazed over as he looked up at the sky. The clouds were thick but a breeze was coming up and the sparks from the fire were making me nervous. It was after the story, the look of the sky and with Hunter arriving that I had wished for only a moment that I hadn't made plans to travel through the woods to the old house.

13

WHAT WAS THAT?

MOST OF THE CAMPERS piled into only a couple tents, even though there was several extra. Hunter and his group were pleased to have their own sleeping quarters. We all disappeared into the tents for the night no doubt with ghosts on our minds.

Mack and I had picked a tent that was on the outside edge of the tenting area. Once we zipped the closing shut I turned to look towards Mack. He was already starting to climb into his sleeping bag.

"What are you doing?"

Mack looked towards me with the color draining from his face. He opened his mouth but said nothing. He puffed out a blast of air then started to stumble over his words, "You heard the story. Well… well I don't think we should try to find the old house." His fingers were digging into the thickness of the sleeping bag. He licked his lips and once more slouched down under the covers.

"The key word here is story. It's just a story." I continued to stand there gazing at Mack. He, on the other hand, was trying hard not to look my way. I lowered my voice as I said, "There's no such thing as ghosts."

He didn't say anything only punched his flat pillow for more volume. Flopping back down onto the already flat pillow he mocked a sleeping mode.

"I want to see why everything has pointed towards staying away from the island. There's something going on here and I would bet money that Charlie Chip has something to do with the house and those big trucks." I snapped around as I heard a burst of screaming followed by laughter coming from one of the other tents. For some reason I felt a bit on edge but I knew this was our moment. Clenching my teeth together I dropped down with a thud on top of my own sleeping bag. "Fine, fine. If you're too scared then Nyla and I will go it alone. I can do this on my own without either of you..."

Mack lay there still, not saying a word. Outside, it was quieting down with only the odd whispers breaking the silence. We could hear the fire crackle and then not too far away the bushes were being roughed up. I lay on top my bedding and my attention was drawn toward the fire light outside casting a shadow on the side of our tent. Someone was dragging something real heavy between our tent and the fire.

It appeared to be Brian's slouched shape. He was humped over and tugging on something. The shape looked like a body being dragged by one leg. His long hair hung down around his shoulders as he continued to grunt and tug on the leg. Mack pulled back into the sleeping bag now horrified with the sight flashing onto the side of our tent.

I pulled myself up onto my knees and crept towards the flap of the tent door. I took hold of the zipper and holding my breath I unzipped the tent so I could get a better look. I gasped as I dropped back away from the door.

Mack pulled back into the corner of the tent as he starred towards my face. "What is it?" The shadow straightened up for a moment.

I broke into a laugh as I said, "Brian is putting a log on the fire."

Mack swung his hand and hit my arm. I grabbed my arm which was still tender from the ball Hunter spun my way at the ball game.

"I don't think you can burn ghosts." Grabbing my arm I rolled over in laughter and pulled the pillow to my face to muffle the sound.

I lay back down on my sleeping bag and closed my eyes. It had been a long day and somehow I felt like it was only the beginning. The shadow of the fire dancing outside the tent was hypnotizing. Mack and I lay there in silence watching the light flicker on and off. The frogs sang their usual noise mixed with the snap and crackled of the fire for some time. My eyes became heavier as I struggled to stay awake.

I heard an owl hoot very close to the back of our tent making me open my eyes. I noticed that the fire had burned down to a low glow on the side of our tent. I looked towards Mack. The slow rhythm of his breathing told me that he was asleep. Earlier I got the feeling that he didn't really want to go with me; perhaps it was just as well. It was bad enough that I was going to sneak out into the night but I could be getting him into a lot of trouble.

I rubbed my eyes and hoped it wasn't too dark. Once more I pulled the tent open and crept out into the silence of the normal night noises. The tents were huddled around the edge of the fires glow. I noticed a lump curled into a fetal position, it was Brian. There was no movement as I stepped with great care around the edge of the bubble of light created by the glowing embers.

Picking up a small stone I lightly tossed it towards Nyla's tent. I looked up above and could see a large moon and scattered clouds. The light breeze was pushing the clouds over the moon every now and then. For the most part I felt I could make my way around the darker shadows towards a path. I looked in the distance at the taller trees. I bent and picked another stone, this time I tossed it with a slight more thrust at the side of her tent. I looked back towards the waters' edge where the trees appeared to be larger, inland they were somewhat smaller.

Nyla looked sleepy as she rubbed the puffiness from her eyes. Twisting her hoodie down to cover the gap between her top and pants she moved quietly. I pushed the bushes to one side as I took a deep breath. The area wasn't really thick with bushes but the tall spruce trees were scattered everywhere with their long dark arms reaching out towards my shoulders. I could feel Nyla's fingers grasping my arm then the back of my neck with her cold fingertips. I shuttered and pulled my sweater up around my ears.

We crept along among the trees until I thought I could see a bit of a clearing ahead. It was an old road, well used. I looked at the soft mud on the edge of the road. There were large fresh tire tracks. Then we could hear something behind us in the bushes so I jumped to one side dragging Nyla along. We crouched low behind a choke cherry bush hanging in long juicy clumps. I held my breath as I watched another shape crawl out from under a bush. It only took me a few seconds to realize that it was Mack.

In a low whisper I said, "I thought you didn't want to come."

Mack jumped as he swung his arms into the air around him. "Dear God man, you scared the liven bee-jesus out of me." Turning a slight color of red was still noticeable in the moonlight. Embarrassed by his reaction in front of Nyla, he dropped his arms and slouched as he looked around the bushes and spied the road only steps away.

"Sorry. I didn't mean to scare you but I wasn't sure who was following us."

"There's no worry, no one in their right mind would be out here wandering around this time of night. I mean except us and maybe a ghost or two."

His eyes shifted around then up above to the now half covered moon. "I woke and noticed you were gone. Never let it be said that I would let my friends go somewhere without my protection." His eyes settled on Nyla once more but soon shifted away from her returned stare.

We walked on along the edge of the road stopping every now and then. The island itself wasn't too wide and I felt like we would be able to walk the width in about fifteen minutes. The trees in the center of the island were huge dead spruce trees with blackened branches stretching overhead. We stayed close to the edge of the road where we would be able to take cover easier.

We walked for some time around and around till I noticed an area where the ground was covered with large gnarly roots. The funny part was I knew I had passed this same set of gnarly roots twice before.

"Somehow the road is going around in circles."

Mack looked up at the sky as the clouds covered the moon one more time. "I think we'll have to follow the road but watch to see where it cuts off again."

I wiped my forehead with the back of my hand. "Ok. I think we should go this way first."

We started off at a good clip, relieved that we at last had a plan. The road in spots was rutted up pretty bad. "Looks like one of those big trucks got stuck here before." The slight breeze had started to become more of a bother. I felt chilled and it was about this time I noticed a noise in the distance. We all scampered to the side of the road and huddled under an extra high bush. I could feel the heat coming off Mack as he puffed a few more hot breaths. Nyla crouched behind us both with her boney fingers digging into my shoulder plus her teeth were chattering. Then the shadow of a truck came into focus. Someone was driving without any lights on.

Two large burly men were pressed into the cab. They only drove another twenty feet before coming to a stop. One of the men with a deeper than deep voice said, "I think this is the same spot we were at last time."

The other man sounded tired and annoyed. He said, "Yea, don't matter much."

They both got out of the truck and pulled a tarp off the back end of the truck. One of the men jumped up on the back. He was working hard as he started to grunt and push at something. Before long we could tell they were dumping some green liquid off the edge of the road. They laughed at some foreign joke and continued at their work.

I motioned towards Mack to back up farther into the bushes. Before long we were out of their range. "Let's go this way. I'm sure the house is more in this area and besides the truck came from over in that direction."

We picked our way back towards the other side of the island. Nyla walked directly behind me, with Mack bringing up the rear. Then suddenly Mack slipped and yelled out. We both turned to look at him as he disappeared from our sight.

I pushed past Nyla who was standing frozen to the spot and jumped towards him. "Mack, what is it?"

The clouds parted and for the first time we had a clear look at a pond of sorts. The top had a look of jelly and was glistening in the moonlight. I dropped to my knees and reached my hand towards Mack. Nyla was now reaching as far as she could from the other side of a large tree.

"Grab my hand, grab my hand."

Mack tried to grip my hand but it was no use. "Get a stick or something. Hurry up, get me out of here. Hurry up!"

Nyla stayed on her knees as she said, "Hang in there Mack. Hang in there. Hurry up Sam."

I twisted around to find a branch lying under a half dead looking maple tree. I grabbed the branch quickly and pushed the end towards Mack. His hands grabbed the branch and I began to pull backwards. It was a slow process but in the end

Mack was sprawled out on the dry ground only feet away from a dumping pit.

I stood above him and looked down. "What is that stuff?"

"I don't know but it burns. Oh no, it's burning my skin." He jumped up and started to tug at his clothing. He groaned in agony as I helped to pull his t-shirt off. I turned his shirt inside out and proceeded to wipe the goo from his arms.

"Oh my God! It feels like glue."

Nyla for the first time looked scared as she brushed the tears away from her face. Her hands only lingered on her ears for a moment.

Mack's eyes looked big and filled with fear. I must have looked horrified because he kept gazing at my face. I couldn't believe it, what was this stuff?

"There I think that's all of it."

"No it can't be because my skin is still burning. Sam make it stop, it's burning." He started to dance in nothing more than his underwear and for the first time wasn't even considering the fact Nyla was standing before him.

Mack was looking even more frantic and then I said, "We're not too far from the house I'm sure of it. Maybe we can get help there."

Nyla said, "No, we should take him back to camp, to Sadie."

It only took me a moment to decide. "No, we're closer to the old house and there's a road there over the sand bar. Besides we can't carry his weight that far, through the woods."

Mack started to scratch his arms as he looked at Nyla. "My legs feel like spaghetti. I don't know how far I can go."

"Put your arm over our shoulders we'll help you." Mack swung his arm up over my shoulder then over Nyla. We started out at a good clip but before long I grew tired with the weight of his body pulling down on me. Then he started to shiver. I stopped, pulling my hoodie off and put it over Mack's shoulders. This was when the moonlight shone out bright enough that I could see a rash on his shoulders and neck. His face looked puffy and his breathing was labored.

"It's not far now Mack, hang in there. Nyla can stay with you in the building till I can get help." We stepped out of the thickest bushes and realized we were only about twenty feet from the back of the house. There was a door hanging by one hinge. Mack slumped down by the base of a maple tree and made no more effort to move.

I sprinted towards the house pushing the door aside to find another door only two feet away. It appeared to be stuck so I put my shoulder up against it. A few more heavy grunts and the other door pushed open. The moonlight shone in through the only window in the room. This was when I noticed the window had steel bars on it. I turned and ran out to help Nyla bring Mack inside.

"Come on buddy. I found a place where you'll be safe till help comes." It was a hard job to get Mack that last twenty feet. Once we tugged him into the room he fell in a hump on the floor.

"Mack, Mack. Can you hear me? Nyla slapped his face then took his pulse. "He was still alive but not responding."

Panic filled every empty spot within my soul. The fact that Mack was laying on the floor, because of me, was over-whelming.

There was one other door in the room. There was a slight flicker of light from under the door. I put my ear up to the wood and listened. It was very faint but as I tried to stop breathing I knew without a doubt someone was in the next room. Then outside I could hear a truck pull up to the front of the house. A scrapping noise of chairs on the floor was followed by heavy footsteps of someone moving around.

I backed away from the door as Nyla sat beside Mack. She said in a low whisper, "Who's there? Will they help us?"

14

WHAT'S NEXT

I COULD MAKE OUT two men talking and they sounded tired and impatient. "When's the boss getting here?"

"I don't know, before long. I talked to him and he said this would be the last dump. We're moving out."

"How come, this is a great area?"

"Too many nosey people like that old man."

"What are we doing with him?"

"He's not long for this world. We'll dump the body after we get away from here."

This was bad, real bad. I twisted my hands together and looked back toward Mack still a large lump on the floor. I rushed to his side. He looked lifeless. A shiver of fear started my insides to shaking.

"Mack, can you hear me? I'm going for help. There are some men in the next room so I want you to be real quiet. Do you understand me? I don't want them to find you here. Stay quiet, ok."

Nyla stepped between me and the door. "I'm the runner and it's my job." Her eyes sparkled with a green light. She reached up to touch my shoulder and in that instant a heat was generated inside me.

She must have read the concern on my face so she added, "I know the way. Don't worry about me. I wouldn't take long."

"What about those holes? It's dangerous to go it alone."

She tipped her head to one side then commented, "And it's not dangerous for you?" With that Nyla twisted to look at Mack one more time. "Past the three pines then turn left over the gnarly roots, twenty feet and then run up the road twenty more feet to the right then turn left. The path is flattened down and not far from the camp. Sadie will know what to do."

When I opened the door for Nyla I noticed the moonlight was gone and it had started to rain. It looked black outside and the trees rustled in the distance. Nyla sprinted past me before I had time to protest. The back of her head soon disappeared into the darkness. I shut the door and returned to Mack's side.

Mack's face and neck were a scarlet red. His eyes were swollen almost shut. Every now and then I could see a slight flicker of his eyelashes. I pulled my hoodie up around his shoulders and said in a shaky voice, "Nyla went for help. Mack started to move no doubt to protest but then slumped back down. She'll be back as soon as possible. I'm sorry man. Sorry to have gotten you two into this."

I moved closer to the door and tried to make out what was being said in the next room. The floor boards were very spongy. I had to move real careful and try not to put much weight in any one spot. I stood close to the door but gazed towards the window hole now dripping steadily with the rain. The hair on the back of my neck stood up as I heard something by the back door. I moved closer to Mack and watched the door as the rain started to splash on the floor beyond Mack's feet.

I could hear footsteps as someone entered the back door of the porch. My first thought was perhaps that Nyla had come back. I pulled myself up from the floor and moved towards the door when Hunter burst into the room. I was stunned with his arrival and was lost for words. Quickly I put my finger to my lips to silence him.

Hunter lifted his nose higher in the air. He brushed the burrs off his pant legs. His eyes moved over the lump on the floor and appeared to widen in size. "What are you doing here?"

"I could ask you the same thing." I stepped closer to Mack and dropped down beside him.

"I heard Mack leaving the camp earlier. First I figured he went to the bathroom but then he didn't come back. It made me wonder what he was up to, so I followed him."

"Did you see Nyla?"

"Yes. She was making enough noise to scare the life out of anything within fifty yards. I hid as she went by in a blur."

"She went for help. Looks like, they are dumping chemicals or something back in the woods. Mack fell in and had a bad reaction to whatever it was." I looked at Mack then turned to read Hunter's expression. His eyes were bigger than big and for the first time I noticed his guard drop.

Hunter bent down and sniffed before turning his nose up in the air. "I did notice the light reflect off something. I figured it was a brook or a pond among the trees. It does smell like some kind of chemicals."

"I already figured that out. This is your dad's land isn't it?" I narrowed my eyes as I starred towards Hunter.

Hunter pulled his shoulders back. "My dad wouldn't have anything to do with chemicals being dumped. I know that for sure."

"Ya, like he tells you what he's doing all the time."

"I don't imagine he does. The thing is I know he's talking of turning this whole parcel of land over to some wilderness nature park. Why would he do that if he knew this would be discovered?"

I turned towards the door to the other rooms. The voices grew louder and then there was a burst of laughter. I heard something hit the floor hard before the voices stopped. Turning towards Hunter I could see the questions on his face.

"I think they are the people that have been dumping the chemicals. We have to be quiet until Nyla brings back some help."

Hunter now knelt down beside Mack and then looked back towards me. "I think he's getting worse. We should try to get him back to the camp." He paused as he realized that Mack was starting to shiver. "Where are his clothes?"

When he looked back towards me with a funny look I said, "His clothes were burning his skin."

Hunter shook his head and grabbed Mack by the arm. "Come on this is going to take awhile. There's a reason I call him big Mack."

I went to the other side and started to help Mack up with assistance from Hunter.

I heard a door shut from somewhere in the front of the building. The voices in the other room were getting louder. I grew more nervous because I knew they were very close to our door.

The person they called boss must have arrived back and things were starting to happen. It sounded like the big guys were beating someone to a pulp. A familiar voice was mixed with the scuffle. The voice was someone I knew. It was someone from the camp.

In the tussle outside our little room the noise became more demanding and once more we heard a body hit the floor. I looked towards Hunter and whispered, "We got to get out of here."

We had Mack up from the floor and propped up under the arms. Hunter was right, Mack was a big guy. Our attention was drawn once more to the noise in the other room. Someone was being pressed up against the door. I could tell from the creaking of the door that it wasn't going to hold out for very long.

The hinges creaked and the floor sagged very close to the door. I knew that voice and before I could say anything to Hunter the door flew open and fell from the frame.

Charlie Chip's short frame came rushing towards us with blood dripping down his whiskery face. His head thumped into my stomach knocking the wind out of me. I stumbled backward as my hands released my hold on Mack. Hunter grunted as Mack's weight overpowered his hold dropping him like a sack of potatoes to the floor.

Almost instantly Hunter jumped to his feet. "What the hell is going on here?"

I watched as Charlie Chip sprawled before my feet. His hands were tied behind his back and his body once more went limp as he passed out. My eyes were drawn up to the face of the boss. There before me stood John. His smile was twisted at an odd angle across his face.

"Well who do we have here?" He pointed towards me and Hunter and nodded at his two lumbering truckers. One of the truckers grabbed my arm and said in a slow drawl of a voice, "What are we… going to do… with them boss?"

The other large man clenched onto the shoulder of Hunter's shirt. I could tell this action wasn't being taken lightly by Hunter. The redness of his face was growing to a color of purple.

"Take you hands off me you stupid thug. My father owns all this land and you will all be arrested and sent to jail."

Hunter continued to jerk at his coat then finally twisted around and planted a fist into the ample gut of the man holding onto him. The man doubled over and grunted as the air burst out of his mouth. This was all I needed.

Hunter yelled, "Run Sam, run."

While everyone's attention was drawn to Hunter and the trucker I made my move. Placing both my hands on the chest of the other trucker I threw all my weight against him. He started stumbling backwards stepping on John who was also looking towards Hunter.

I sprinted out the door leading to the front of the house. It was the closest way out. John made a lunge to grab me. The trucker was trying to collect himself as he became tangled between John and me.

As I left the room behind me I ran through a small room and headed down the hallway. At the end of the hallway there were three doors I picked the one on the right. It was an old kitchen with some broken chairs which littered the large room. Standing behind the framework of the door, I listened.

John grunted then yelled at the trucker. "Get the hell out of my way."

He rushed into another small room then stopped likely to look out the crumbling window to see no sight of me. Then he picked something up from the floor and his steps were getting closer. He picked the door opposite the one I went through. I could hear his footsteps moving away from me now. In the distance I heard Hunter making loads of racket with the other truckers. This was my time to move it.

I crept quietly towards the only other door in the room. It was an old back stairway from the kitchen to the bedrooms upstairs. The narrow steps forced me to focus on each one. The small area was filled with dust and cobwebs. I gradually climbed the stairway praying that the steps would hold my weight.

I could hear John yelling something in the other room. His voice was getting louder as he drew closer. It sounded like he hit the wall with a stick as he continued to listen for any movement on my part.

"Come on Sam. You might as well come out. You're wasting time. We need to get Mack to a doctor." He swung with the stick and hit the wall on the other side of where I stood.

I tried to be as quiet as I could, slowly one step at a time. When he hit the wall once more I gasped, holding my breath. There were several boards missing but I could easily step over them. Then I turned in response to John's voice behind me.

"I see you. Come on Sam. Come back and let's talk about this."

"No. You've been dumping chemicals all along. What have you done to Charlie Chip? I know you wouldn't let us go now?"

With those final words John made a lunge to grab me. A few of the boards under his feet broke. I picked up speed to get to the top. Pulling the cobwebs off my face I looked around. I was now in a small room above the kitchen. It had one window hole and a small opening with no door.

The rain was dripping through one corner of the roof where I could easily see the lightning in the distance. The thunder rumbled and I wondered for only a second how Nyla was doing. How long would I have to hold John off? I needed to keep them here at all costs.

15

JUMP OR BE PUSHED

Below where I stood I could tell John was running to the main stairway. I moved to the next room which had an opening in the side of the wall. The floor was missing close to the edge of what was likely a window. I could hear the thump of John's steps getting closer so I darted into the next room. It was a large room with the remains of an old bed, feather tick and all. In the middle of the floor was a table laying on its side. Broken beer bottles and old tin cans with rusty edges were scattered across the floor.

The room was a good lookout point with an open doorway leading to a balcony. The roof in the corner of the room was totally gone. The lightning flashed at that moment showing me the floor appeared to be intact. The rain drummed down on the balcony which was hanging with a tilt towards the ground. The old railing didn't look any better than the floor. Slowly I stepped towards the balcony. Holding onto the only solid piece of wood by the edge I turned to see John entering the room. He gripped a large stick with his right hand.

Walking towards me with no smile on his face he bent and picked up a bottle. "Well, my oh my. You've got yourself into quite a pickle now don't you Sammy boy." He moved closer as he continued to talk, swinging the club from one side to the other. "Thank you for helping me out. You see it's going to look like you boys were hurt when exploring an old house you were all told to stay away from."

"What about Charlie Chip? How will you explain him?" I tightened my grip on the wall as the rain started to run down my arm to my elbow.

"Charlie Chip, he's nothing more than an under-cover cop, a bad one at that, but still too close. I'll dispose of him somewhere else." He laughed a well practiced laugh and then with a flash of speed he hurled the bottle at my head. The sharp edge sliced through my t-shirt into my shoulder as I ducked to one side. I could feel the warm blood run down my arm and drip off my elbow.

In a low voice John asked, "Do you want to jump or should I push ya?"

John moved from one side to the other beyond the table. Dropping the stick he bent once more and collected a few more bottles. He laughed again as he wound up with another broken bottle. The moment the bottle left his hand I dropped down to the smooth floor boards.

The glass bottle sailed over my head. Right behind it he threw another bottle. This one caught me on the knee cap. It didn't break but sent a sharp pain up my leg. The thunder rumbled outside with the lightning flashing only seconds later. The boards where I stood were getting slippery. I lunged to the other side of the doorway.

John grabbed for me as I reached for the other side of the door frame. My foot slipped as I grasped at the wooden frame. He clutched the edge of my t-shirt as he started to lose his balance. With my fingers digging into the soggy frame I kicked at him with the flat of my foot. It was just enough. The whole balcony started to teeter. Even in the dim light I could see John's mouth drop open.

Letting go of my shirt John clawed at the edge of the door just as the whole thing dangled from the side of the house. The bulging eyes and blank look came with the realization that he was going down. It only took seconds before the dilapidated balcony hit the ground.

I stood on the edge and looked down. The rain thundered down even harder blurring my vision but still I could see John's unconscious body twisted among the splintered wood.

A loud clap of thunder rumbled above my head mixing with the sound of sirens. In the distance I could see lights flashing as they made their way over the sand bar towards the house. Nyla had made it through. Once more looking down at John I turned and made my way back through the maze of doorways to the back room where Mack and Hunter were being held.

The two truckers looked stunned as I stepped through the doorway. One of the men grabbed my arm. I yanked my arm from his grip as I said, "It's over you guys. John is out of commission. The cops are here."

They looked at each other and made a beeline for the back door. I didn't care anymore. I looked at Mack who resembled an oversized marshmallow.

"Thanks for the help." I smiled at Hunter. He nodded.

I dropped down to my one good knee and spoke to Mack, "Hey buddy. Help is on the way, hang in there." I paused as I collected my thoughts then spoke in a very low voice, "I'm really sorry I got you into all this." All I could see now was the slight flicker of Mack's eyelashes. His skin was puffy and peeling in spots. All I could hear was his labored breathing.

Then my eyes were drawn to his hand as he lifted one thumb up. The guilt I felt consumed me. My feelings were mixed as I experienced one of my worst moments with one of my most memorable. Someone else had been hurt and was suffering all because of me.

Sadie rushed into the room and knelt down by Mack. Then she took notice of Charlie Chip still sprawled out on the floor. Sadie spoke softly to Mack. Words I couldn't even hear. Once more I could see the flicker of Mack's eyelashes.

Sadie raised her voice now and said, "Charlie can you hear me, Charlie."

Then I could see Charlie's hand starting to move. He grunted as he very slowly pulled himself up straighter. Patches of dried blood covered his neck and face and he cradled his left arm.

Sadie's face was creased with lines as she once more repeated, "Charlie, are you alright?"

His voice cracked as his usual raspy noise sputtered out, "Yea, I'm ok. You take care of that young fellow. How did you find me?"

Sadie said, "It was your lucky night. Sam sent Nyla for help."

The paramedics moved in fast and with great care worked around Mack and Charlie. Time dragged as I waited. Sadie cleaned and bandaged my cut before they moved Mack and Charlie out the door.

Nyla had been pushed back to the wall from Mack's side as she made room for the medics. After noticing Hunter she ran her hand up over her hair, still in the state of being stubble. When she spoke a chill was very noticeable. "Where did you come from?"

I stepped between them and said, "He was going to help me with Mack." I looked towards Hunter but his chin was turned up into the air once more. He shrugged his shoulders as he pushed his hands into his pockets.

I said to them both, "Nyla you saved the day, not only for Mack but for Charlie Chip. I also want to thank you Hunter for your help."

Hunter looked my way and then before I could say anything else he said, "I wouldn't want anyone to get hurt on my father's land even if you had no business snooping around."

I stepped closer to Nyla and placed my hand on her shoulder to restrain her before she could tackle Hunter.

Nyla blurted out, "Since when did you guys become such good friends? If my memory serves me right you never liked him."

"Well I have to admit when I'm wrong. I'm glad he was here and I'll never forget what he did. You know even the worst of people are not bad all the way through."

Nyla looked towards me, tugged her earring, shook her head then walked away. Hunter was likely still a jerk but there was a ray of hope somewhere inside him. Perhaps I was the only one who saw it.

The back door swung open as two police officers appeared out of the darkness with the two truckers in cuffs. I stood in the doorway and watched as the cops stuffed the larger than large men through the doorway.

When I reached the front door I looked to one side gazing at the broken pieces of the balcony. Apparently John had already been taking by ambulance. The rain had stopped leaving the air with a stale musty aroma. The stars were sparkling here and there around the dark clouds.

I thought to myself, how glad I was that Mack was on his way to the hospital. A chill ran over my body as I remembered Mom saying to me, 'even seasoned cops get hurt.' I was the reason that Mack was hurt. Inside I felt like my big mystery days were over. I realized in that moment it's not always about me. I don't live in a bubble. The people that I carry with me are always in dangers way. It could have been me on the stretcher and the truth be known I wished it had have been.

Trouble was it was one of my best friends. I knew now deep inside I would never be able to do this to another person. Mack had followed me down the path blindly and I wasn't able to save him. He was doing nothing more than following his friend. I felt Mack would be ok but still even seasoned cops get hurt. I was playing in the big world and would never be able to take things so lightly again.

I realized that Mack would not have wanted to stay behind and at that moment it was indeed his choice. Still I had led him into the face of danger knowing more about the chances than he did. I ran my hand up over my hair that had now completely grown over my stitches. The pain my mother must have felt, the worry, the despair in hoping it would never happen again.

Summer camp ended the next day and our canoe race never happened. The area was marked for a cleanup. The camp would be opened again next year. I felt pretty good about my time spent at camp. Nyla assured me that she would be back next summer come hell or high water. Hunter kept his distance but I had glimpsed the real heart of Hunter. I would never hate Hunter that way again. He was simply another young man trying to be noticed, trying to be special and he was all that and more. I knew the real Hunter.

The last time I saw Hunter he held his chin up high. As he got closer he snorted then said, "Next year at the canoe challenge, I'm going to kick your ass."

I stopped for only a moment before replying, "In your dreams." I smiled and walked away. When I turned and looked his way one last time I could see it, a slight smile that turned the corner of his mouth up. We had turned another corner and deep down we would always have a certain amount of respect for each other from that day on.

Dad arrived to take me back to Hopeville later that same day. There were no speeches on the way back as to what I should or shouldn't have done. I learned how much my father thought of me that day. The trust that he had in me to understand what was right. Mom didn't say much because I'm sure she could see the concern on my face.

Dad patted my back and said in a lower than usual tone, "You did good son, Mack will be ok. Things have a way of settling down and next year will be better."

Arriving home a few weeks earlier than usual meant I would be more help in the moving process. I was given more time to have closure with my childhood years. I was ready to move on beyond the time of Hanna Rae and the mysteries that consumed us for years.

I kept in touch with Mack since he was in the hospital until given a clean bill of health. Hunter did pay Mack a visit a couple of times and still let on he was doing it for his father. Mack said he could hear everything that went on that night. He explained to Nyla how Hunter liked to play the part of being tough.

Within the next couple weeks I was ready for the move to Onslow and looked forward to being closer to my new found friends. Somehow during that time at camp I realized how we all struggle with relationships. I was for the first time looking forward to having my father around. I had found with the moving process that Dad relied on me more and treated me differently, more like a grown up person.

The day we moved the last of our things from Hopeville was somehow sad. There had been several trips with our belongings. When I first walked into my own room in the large house I was struck by the warmth of the sun that now poured into my room from the large bay window that aimed towards the sunset.

I turned to see Dad and Mom standing together in the doorway, both smiling. "This used to be your father's room when he was your age." Mom's hand was on the wooden frame of the doorway and tears filled her eyes. I stepped towards her and that was when I saw it.

"Your father felt this would make you feel more like a part of this home. We never have to lose the parts of our past that were special."

There nailed to the wall was the wooden door frame from the old home. The gouges were rough and one side was JC and the other was me.

"He thought perhaps this would help."

I looked at the wood and ran my fingers over the marks and smiled towards his reddened face. He started to stutter as he tried to get it out, "I hope you like it. I've taken the liberty to pick something else up for you." He reached his hand out passing a leather strap towards me. "Give it a tug."

I felt the leather smooth within my grasp. I looked at their faces, both smiling. I gave the strap a tug and something pulled back. A thumping of large feet in the hallway took me by surprise. A red haired Irish setter pup came bouncing around the corner. He was no more than five months old. His feet appeared to be larger than any other portion of his body. His long tail had the hair twisted around and around. His long floppy ears were covered with the silkiest hair I had ever felt.

I dropped to my knees and hugged the neck of my newest best friend. It did feel good because for the first time in my life I felt like this was home and we were all a family now.

The End